After The Pain

DAVID CAINES

Order this book online at www.trafford.com
or email orders@trafford.com

Most Trafford titles are also available at major online book retailers.

Printed in the United States of America.

ISBN: 978-1-4269-5049-0 (sc)
ISBN: 978-1-4269-5050-6 (hc)
ISBN: 978-1-4269-5051-3 (e)

Library of Congress Control Number: 2010918032

Trafford rev. 12/16/2010

 www.trafford.com

North America & international
toll-free: 1 888 232 4444 (USA & Canada)
phone: 250 383 6864 ♦ fax: 812 355 4082

Dedication
For My Mother

Pearlie Caines

In Memory Of
Shawn
1970-2005

...Death is decidedly overwhelming to say the least, but a greater force called love prevails long after the agony of loss starts to ebb. It is not a coincidence that we are instructed early on to love, and to follow the example of our Master as he stood at the tomb of a beloved friend and "moaned in the Spirit," because of the love that he held for that family. Death is overwhelming...but is a mere shadow in the light of love.

DC

A very special thanks to the following friends and family for all that you have done to make this journey a little bit easier. I will be forever grateful.

Alice Gibbs, Deborah Barrows, Steve and Sheila Strider, Kayla Strider, Alerth and Janice Young, Darnell Gatling, Verly and Barbara Smith, Annette Caines, Linda Washington and Najee Pitts, Edwin and Yvonne Kennedy, Olliver Davis, Fred and Chastain Pitts, Darlene Grant, Mary Byrd, Debra Mack, Carl Keyes, Dr. Peter White, Dr. Mark Polatnick, Mary J. Williams, Essie Styles, Belinda Haynes, Stephanie Payne Monroe, Ernestine Hadley, Bert Pope-Matthews, Fredrick Brown, Sharon Johnson, Cedric Robinson, Eleanor Lamb, Vickie Moore, Iva Allison, Henry Brown, Byron Bobb, Harold and Delores Allen, Annie and George Myers, Jackman, Johnnie M. Jackson, Bernadine Silvers, Todd Halstead, Mary Reed, Gene and Rayna Bittel, Harold Stinson, Andre and Andrea Silvers, Barbara Schely, James Folston, Darnell Epps, Valerie Carter, Mr. and Mrs. Henry L. Fuqua, Thomas and Mary Stinson, Ola Pollard, Peachie Kirlew, Kenneth Laster, Michael Downes and Doris Wiems, Howard and Jackie Tyson, Raghbir Singh, Eulious and Pauline Stinson, Patricia Walker, rjo Winch, Eileen Jones, Evelyn Wallace, Leverne Mott, Bernard McArthur, Z. DeCarish, Marsh and Shawndricka Gardner, Earl Stevens, LaVonda McQuinton, Ricky Reed, Beverly Colvin, Fannie Fredricks, Jackie Powell, Victor Caines, Faye Hurston-Weatherington, Pastor Frances Weaver, Zandra Whatley.

You were strong when I could not be.

Autumnal 1968

Late autumn, cold, bare trees, hard; the harvest long over. The days are short; the nights are long. So very long! This is not the season of love, and yet, I found you. Was this an omen of how life would be? For in here, this season, we are taught that death must be.

As my end fastly approaches, I've given myself over to this time to tell you that through it all, I've loved you without boundries. The only thing that I would consider a tragedy is the possibility that when this is all over, I won't be allowed in the place where you now reside. Our Lord, don't do that to me!

From the moment that I rested my eyes upon you, I knew that I loved you. Tonight I dreamed of you, and I told you that I loved you and kissed you. I woke up and I thought of the day that I kissed your hand over and over. (You made me do it!) But I was a willing subject! My stomach churns in angst as I remember the terrible feeing of losing you.

I had found a new love even before you left. I don't know why, it was just that way. I wonder if I decided to love someone else, or were the charms so that I could not resist? I have not knowledge of it, but it was a mistake that I still regret. Had things not changed, we would have had the dreams of young love to contend with for more than just one night…more than just two? Perhaps there would be no need to write this ode.

As I often think, when things have gone awry, that I would lie upon your grave and slowly fade into where you are. I'm hungry for knowing-did you think of me as you left? Did you feel the warmth of my tears, or were they just cold drops of water on the nights of rain? A lifetime of loss and pain will now cease to be; I will cry no more for wanting and loving you. And if our God loves us as he has promised, then to you, I'll always be.

Spring. Rebirth, new life, Love. The blossoming of flowers and trees, and a young man's fancy....But it couldn't be, because my love was laid to rest beneath the now full trees.

DC

1

Dessie sat on the beach burying her toes in the sand; the Sea lulling her to a place of peace and stillness. Could all of this be real? She thought to herself, life had not been so cruel. But she knew that it had been. Just over a month ago, she had lost her lover, her cousin, and gained a brother in that exact order. She yearned for any semblance of a normal life that had been hers so many, many days ago. Had it not been for her friends, she feared that she would have soon taken the step that even now she still contemplated. They're pushing her to take a week's vacation to this beautiful island was the best thing that she could have done. Staying at home feeling miserable and unwanted was too depressing.

Soon after Junie Boy's funeral, she realized that staying in her current job would be a mistake; seeing that it would somehow always tie her to Ray. She wanted to be free of him. She gave her two-week's notice just a few days after returning. She felt so beat down that all she wanted to do was stay home in bed. She needed time to think about what it was that she wanted to do about the situation she was now faced with. She had to make up her mind quickly. The baby growing inside of her will swell her belly in a couple of months, and everybody would know. She wished that Junie Boy was still alive. He always had the answers. The one thing that she was certain of though; was that she had to leave Westfield. There was no way that she could stay there and withstand all the stares and the gossip that would surely follow. Ruthie didn't deserve the shame that Dessie was sure she would feel.

DC

When Dessie quit her job, Ruthie asked why, and she couldn't tell her. It should have been the most natural thing in the world for any woman to go to her mother and tell her that she was pregnant, but all Dessie felt like doing was hiding; knowing full well that she wouldn't be able to do it forever. Before she left for Jamaica, Ruthie made her a cream colored pantsuit, and commented on her breast and hip increases.

"I just sit around eating a bunch of junk food Mama," Dessie said, trying to pass it off as nothing to worry about.

"I hope this trip gets you outside and doing some of that exercising stuff that you see on the television when folks go to these fancy places."

"I am Mama," Dessie said, "I'll probably get so much sun, I'll come by here and you won't even recognize me." Dessie said.

"I'll recognize you no matter what," Ruthie told her, "a mama always knows her chillun."

Dessie wouldn't respond to her mother's comment, and was glad that her back was to her when she spoke.

"So, when do you plan to start looking for another job?" Ruthie asked.

"I want to leave my options open for a while. Working in the corporate world is too hectic for me right now," Dessie explained.

"I thought you said you worked for the business," Ruthie said, sounding confused.

"Business' and 'corporate' means the same thing Mama." Dessie explained.

"Well folks needs to settle on one thing and call it that! Do you want me to do your hair before you leave?" Ruthie asked her daughter.

"No Mama. I'm going to get it braided so I won't have to worry about it once I'm there."

"What you gonna do about your place since you ain't working now?"

"I still have a couple of months already paid for," Dessie told her, "I might find another job here and won't have to move anytime soon." Dessie knew that she was just making up things to say to keep Ruthie from finding out the truth.

Ruthie had already seen that Ray was no longer involved with Dessie. Reverend C.L. had announced the previous Sunday that Ray and Barbara Bolland were the new parents of a baby girl. When Ruthie had mentioned it to Dessie over the phone, no emotion came across the phone line, but bitter tears Ruthie couldn't see were falling. All Dessie could think about was that that baby was going to live a privileged, soft life, but this other child needed the same entitlements. They are both of the same blood!

"I'm so glad that you came to your senses and left that man alone. You can find somebody way better than that," Ruthie affirmed to Dessie, who made no comment.

Ray had called Dessie a few days after Junie Boy's funeral to ask if she was still pregnant. She wouldn't tell him anything, and that whatever choice she had made had nothing to do with him. He had sounded nervous and scared, and he needed to be. He wasn't sure if she had gone through with the abortion or not.

"If you ever come near me or my family, I will do any and everything to protect them Dessie!" Ray threatened.

"Ray you don't know what I have on your sorry ass! I regret the day that I met you! The Department of Labor would love to hear how you forced me into a sexual relationship, and when I became pregnant, you gave me two thousand dollars to get rid of it. The doctor that you sent me to, could be summoned to testify at trial. Now do you want to push me Ray?" Dessie demanded. The line was silent for a few seconds. "I didn't think so!" Dessie said, and hung up the phone.

But what she couldn't hang up was her heart. She was hurt by feelings of love that still seemed to plague her; so when these tried to manifest themselves, she forced herself to remember what he had so coldly done to her, and what she had allowed him to do.

DC

"Taking this vacation will do you a lot of good." Ruthie said.

"I hope so Mama. I really do hope so. Since Junie Boy got killed, I really don't have anyone that I feel close to here. Tasha is in medical school. We hardly ever see each other anymore."

"Reverend C.L. and Charlene are coming over this evening to visit. They want to talk to me about keeping Tyquan and the new baby when it gets here. Why don't you come over too? Reverend C.L. would love to see you."

"Mama, I just can't do it right now. I mean, Clanford knew all along that he was Daddy's son. He could have told us. If he was afraid, he could have still told us when daddy died."

"Dessie, I just don't blame it on him. He didn't make his self. It ain't his fault.'" Ruthie pleaded with Dessie.

"But Mama, he was so against Junie Boy who held no secrets, and he walked around with the biggest secret of all!'"

"Everybody has to answer for they own selves in judgement," Ruthie said to an unyielding Dessie. "If the church can see all the good he's done, then I'm sure you can see a splinter of that good. Charlene is married to him, and the mother of his children and she didn't know either," Ruthie explained.

"That's just it Mama! He didn't even tell the woman that he's married to! I would like to believe that the one person in the world that should know everything about you; does! But he didn't even tell her! There's too much deceit involved to look at it as something that's private."

"But Dessie, we all have to forgive if we want to be forgiven. You have to think about that."

Dessie didn't feel very comfortable discussing Clanford and changed the subject.

"Have you heard from Aunt Beatrice, Mama?" Dessie inquired.

"Yeah, she calls me when she's so drunk and thinks that everybody is out to get her money. She actually sat out on the porch for three days and nights waiting on the mailman to bring her the check from the insurance company. Now she done started telling me that one of her friends and Wesley has been messing around. Said she played like she was sleep when this woman got there, and instead of her leaving when Wesley told her that she was sleep, he and the woman was out on the sun porch together. She keeps on talking about putting him out, but he ain't going nowhere 'fo that money do."

"Mama I used to think that Junie Boy was crazy to leave Aunt Beatrice all that money, but maybe it was just what she needed to do herself in." Dessie said.

"Don't talk that old foolishness Dessie Lee! Junie Boy loved his Mama; she just ain't never had no time for him. Poor Patrice has to do just about everything, and for everybody! Since that child finished school, she ain't been no morn' a slave for Bea, them twins, and Wesley. She tried to tell me something that night of the wake, but Bea made her get out of the kitchen and walk all the way down to that gas station from where they stays just to get her old drunken friends some ice. I told Bea that she must be outta her mind to send that child down that dark road like that. She told me that that was her child and whatever she told her to do, she'd better not waste no damn time getting it done!"

"That's so unfair," Dessie said softly, "she's going to end up leaving just like Junie Boy did.'

"I sort of hope she does," Ruthie said, "God knows she ain't going to get anywhere staying there!" Dessie hugged Ruthie extra tight, telling her that she was glad that it was she who was her mother. Dessie knew that if everything went as she planned, she wouldn't be seeing her mother for quite a while, and it did hurt.

DC

Arriving in Montego Bay was a cultural shock for the four friends. The heat was stifling; getting through customs seemed to take forever. Once they were finally outside, the sights and sounds of this beautiful island amazed them. There seemed to be hundreds of people at the airport. Several guys approached them asking if they needed a cab. They declined their offers by the sheer look of them. They were foreigners, but they weren't stupid. Vicki approached a man she assumed was a police officer dressed in a colorful uniform. Vicki could barely understand what he was saying because of his heavy accent. He signaled to a guy leaning on a car not far from the departure area. She spoke to him for a few seconds telling him where they wanted to go. The taxi guy followed Vicki over to where the others were standing. He automatically started lifting their luggage and placing as much as would fit into the trunk of his car. The two remaining bags were secured on the hood of the car with some rope that he carried with him.

Vicki, Sharon and Debra sat in the back seat, and Dessie got in the passenger seat in the front, and she soon regretted it. The first thing that she noticed was that the steering wheel was on the opposite side of the car from what they were used to. That alone made her not want to drive, but once they got onto the road to take them to the resort, Dessie found out what real fear felt like. The guy had to have been traveling at least eighty miles per hour at his lowest speed! Dessie screamed, covered her face, openly prayed; a look of pure terror on her face.

Dessie was crying and visibly shaken by the time they reached the resort. She started cursing the driver who was already out of the car and getting their luggage.

"Don't you ever come near us again!" Dessie screamed at him; still shaking from the ride and crying while her friends tried to calm her down. "Ya'll don't understand! To see cars coming at you at that speed, and this idiot didn't even try to move over! I didn't come all the way here to die in an accident just because this bastard's ego is in jeopardy!"

"That's why I didn't want to ride in the front seat," Vicki said, "I heard how they drive here."

"You should have at least warned me Vicki!" Dessie said. She started to say something else when her stomach heaved and everything she had for lunch was on the grass. She felt really sick, and it seemed like forever before she stopped throwing up. She was so glad that her friends were there. Without them, she would have been on her knees as weak as she felt. When she stopped heaving and stood up straight, she was surprised to find that it was their driver who had been holding onto her. Dessie squirmed away from him. "You bastard!" Dessie screamed at him, "You could have killed us!"

"Me no kill no one yet!" He said, with a broad smile.

Dessie continued to chastise him, and he and her friends continued to smile.

"Why do ya'll think this is so funny?" Dessie yelled.

"Look pon ya face!" the driver said. Dessie didn't understand. Vicki took her by her hand to the side view mirror of the car where she saw what was causing them to laugh. Her mascara had run down her cheeks, and along with her make-up and lipstick smearing, she looked like a circus clown; which only made her that much madder.

"You're still a bastard!" Dessie said to the driver.

"Me a no such ting! Me mudder and me fodder dey a marry! Me a look pon ya face and tell truth!" Dessie looked to Vicki to decipher what the guy had said.

"He said that his father and mother are married so he can't be a bastard," Vicki interpreted.

"Like hell he ain't!" Dessie hotly replied. Debra and Sharon were busy helping the guy, Danny, retrieve their luggage from the car since he had to get back to the airport to 'run taxi' as he called it. Dessie grabbed her suitcase from Danny the minute he untied it from the luggage rack. Along with her carry on, Dessie struggled on the walkway leading into the resort. She was so weak and queasy she wasn't getting very far. Danny looked on her predicament with an amused smile playing at the corners of his mouth. After a few seconds, he walked over and took the suitcase away from her.

"I can carry my own luggage, thank you!" Dessie said weakly, but still anger tinged.

"Me know ya con; dats why me fi come elp ya!" Dessie was too weak to protest. She followed him absently. Danny placed her suitcase at the counter. As he turned around to leave, he gave Dessie a wide smile and told the others goodbye. He stood in front of Dessie with his dazzlingly white teeth. "Me soon come! We go pon beach to flex!" Dessie got angry all over again.

"Did ya'll hear what that bastard just said to me?" Dessie said with indignation, "He just told me I was going to the beach to have sex with him! That bastard doesn't know me!"

"Take it easy Dessie!" Vicki instructed, "He's just saying that he wants to take you on the beach to relax."

"How do you know what he said Vicki?" Dessie asked.

"There's a lot of West Indians in Brooklyn, and I'm around them a lot, so their dialect and accents are not that foreign to Me.," she explained.

"I still don't want to go to a beach with him." Dessie said, following the others. A resort worker loaded their luggage on a cart as another worker led them to their cottage.

Their cottage was located not too far from the beach. They could stand on the veranda and see the beautiful sea above the lush greenery. The sight was breathtakingly beautiful and serene.

Dessie and Debra took the larger of the two adjoining rooms. Kitchen space was included, which the four of them would share. The first thing that Dessie did when she entered the room was to turn on the air conditioner. The room was stuffy from being closed up, and the heat was starting to make Dessie nauseous. She asked Debra which of the two beds she would prefer and Dessie took the other one; which she crawled onto after washing her face with cool water.

DC

Debra, Sharon and Vicki decided to go hang out at the resort swimming pool, and the three changed into bathing suits. They asked Dessie if she wanted to join them, but she declined the offer; telling them that she was tired and wanted to rest a bit before venturing out. The others grabbed their stuff and left the room.

Dessie laid in the stillness of the now cool room with the sound of soothing reggae music being played from a distance. Soothed by this peacefulness, Dessie was soon sleeping. She dreamed of Ray holding and comforting her; telling her that it was all right and that they were not going to kill their baby. He told her that he was free to marry her and wanted to do it right away, and that he had the wedding party all assembled in the next room. Instantly she was transformed from a sad, broken woman into an enchantingly beautiful bride with a radiant smile. Ray took her by her hand and walked her to the door where the wedding march could be heard loudly announcing their arrival. The happy couple never stopped smiling and looking at each other with all the love their hearts held. Ray reached for the doorknob, and gently placed his arm around his beautiful bride to be, to lead her into the wedding hall. As soon as they stepped into the room, the music stopped and Dessie turned her gaze away from Ray's to see why. What she saw caused her to scream out in agony. Everyone in the room had on surgical masks and wore full surgical gear. They parted in the middle where Ray's wife Barbara stood welcoming Dessie to a table with stirrups. Dessie turned to Ray for protection, and her once happy groom had turned from a handsome hero into something hideous and threatening. He pushed her forward, forcing her to the table. She could see the door that they had come through getting further, and further away from her. All of a sudden, all she could hear was the sound of vacuums. They were as loud as the wedding march had been. Ray continued to push her towards the table with a diabolical laugh that chilled her to the marrow of her bones. He had her at the table, pressing her downward as she screamed.

"Wake up Dessie! Wake up!" Debra demanded, shaking Dessie by the shoulders. Dessie woke up screaming and flinging her arms wildly about her.

"Are you okay Dessie?" Debra asked; stepping back before Dessie's fist connected. It took Dessie a few seconds to realize that she was safe and that it was only a dream. She sat up sweating and shaking. Dessie didn't think that she could feel any sadder than she had been feeling, but the dream seemed to sink her to a new low.

"Are you okay Dessie?" Debra worriedly asked again.

"I'm okay." Dessie assured her friend. Debra seemed to let out a sigh of relief as she sat on the bed, opposite Dessie.

"I hope you aren't still worried about that guy's driving to the point where it's making you have nightmares."

"No. That wasn't it. But I guess my nerves got quite a workout today," Dessie said, to explain away the effect that the dream had had on her.

"We met a couple of guys at the pool who are taking us out to eat tonight. We want to try some of the native cuisine. The resort food is more American style than island. We told them that you were in the room resting, and would probably be joining us for dinner."

Dessie's first impulse was to decline the invitation, but the reason she had let her friends talk her into coming in the first place was to get away from all the stress and heartache she has had to endure these last few weeks. Debra had spoken to Dessie twice before she heard her.

"What did you say Debra?" Dessie asked.

"I asked which dress do you the like the best; the blue or the green?"

"I like the blue one best." Dessie told her. Debra placed the blue dress on the bed and went to prepare for a shower. Dessie reluctantly got up to search through her suitcase to find something suitable to wear for the evening. She chose a white strapless cotton dress. She hunted in both suitcases for her white sandals before she realized that they were beside the bed where she had taken them off.

While she was clipping her braids together to keep them from getting soaked, she caught a glimpse of herself in the mirror and studied it for a moment. Her cheeks were full and alive; skin was clear, but her eyes were not happy. No matter how much she smiled, the sadness remained in them. She caressed her breast. They felt full and soft. Her hips were bigger than they had ever been. She wondered had her friends noticed the changes that she felt were too obvious to ignore. Ruthie hadn't missed them. With that thought, Dessie sat on the bed and buried her head in her hands and wept with the decision she had already made. She knew that it would kill her mother if she ever found out. After a few moments Dessie cleaned her face and promised herself that she was not going to keep on crying. She was going to face whatever decision she had to make with all the courage she could muster.

DC

When everyone was dressed and ready to depart, Dessie suddenly remembered something she had intended to do and told the others that she would catch up to them. Back in the room, Dessie opened her overnight case and unzipped the inside pocket and took out the photograph of Ray that she always carried with her. She took one last look at it, struck a match and ignited it. She watched as it curled up to nothing but a grey-black mass of ashes. She was satisfied with having the courage to part with something she once placed value on. If she could do the same thing with her emotions, she could win the battle. Cleansing herself of him was what she was trying to do. Once she could rid herself of those feelings, she could carry on with the rest of her plans. But her thoughts, as she made her way to the reception area, was everything but cleansing. The baby would forever tie her to Ray whether she was in his life or not; she would always have a daily reminder of him.

When she met up with the others, they all seemed to be paired up with a guy, and automatically she felt as if she were intruding. Dessie stood with her arms folded while Sharon introduced her to the guys they had met earlier. Dessie said a weak hello before quietly retreating to a chair by a large picture window. Dessie glanced over at her friends and wished that she were as happy and carefree as they were. The men, it appeared, were in disagreement about where they would dine. Vicki finally convinced them to take the group to a place that served chicken. Once that was settled, Dessie inquired as to why they were still waiting.

"They're waiting on one of their friends who have the other car. We can't all fit in one Vicki said. Dessie was famished, and hadn't eaten anything since lunch on the plane; then losing it once she had arrived in Montego Bay.

"Ere im a com now!" one of the guys announced to the group. Dessie turned in the direction that everyone had focused his or her attention. Dessie suddenly felt her temperature rising. It was the guy that had picked them up at the airport. Dessie looked sharply at her friends who in turn looked away to avoid her angry look. She wanted to go back to the cabin, but she needed some food badly. She made sure that she did not make eye contact with Daniel. He said hello to everyone, but Dessie acted as if she hadn't heard him. When they headed out, Dessie deliberately walked away from Daniel and his car. She rode in the car that carried Debra and the other two guys. Who she learned were named Fredrick and Clive.

Arriving at the restaurant, Clive motioned For Dessie to sit next to him. She did so reluctantly. She wasn't interested in conversation, but she definitely did not want to sit next to Daniel; who looked rather disappointed when she accepted the seat next to Clive. As the evening wore on, talk turned to seeing the sights on the Montego Bay side of the island.

"We a must go to Santa Cruz!" Fredrick announced.

"Plus, we a show ya where we a from in St. Elizabeth." Clive told the women.

"Maybe me con show you Negril." Daniel said directly to Dessie; who turned her head away from his obvious sexy stare. She had to give it to him though, he wasn't giving up easily. *"I know this fool don't think I'm going to get in another car with him!"* Dessie thought to herself.

"We con stop pon Black River," Clive included, "Me ear a big ting a g'won dere!"

"What is he saying Vicki?" Sharon asked, "you're the only one that understands it." Vicki laughed and told them that she couldn't understand it herself when they spoke fast.

"I think he said something about going to a river."

"I'm not going to go get in anybody's river!" Dessie said strongly. All three men laughed loudly.

"We no mean we a go in river," Danny explained, "The place, town is call Black River." He said, seemingly only to Dessie. She had to admit that out of the three men, Danny was the only one that she really could halfway understand. She attributed that talent to the fact that he was a taxi driver, and probably picked up a lot of fares at the airport. Dessie decided to cut him some slack since he was trying so hard to get her to talk to him. Her eyes softened as she listened to him.

"Fe we justa small island pon de face of dis earth. Me people are poor in money, but rich in culture. To see ow some of we fe live, wood make ya cry. Dats why so many of we won come to America. Fe we work ard fe we money. Fe we can make it betta dere."

Dessie instantly felt sorry for the people, but the small amount of the island that she'd seen so far was astoundingly beautiful. If she lived in a setting such as this, she wouldn't care if she were poor. Her riches would be found in the tranquility of this beautiful island.

After dinner, the men invited the women to go out to a nightclub. Dessie really didn't want to go, but they had all agreed that should one person leave the resort to go out to a nightclub or anything, the others would go as well. She didn't want to spoil the evening for the others, so she went along.

The place the guys chose was called 'Mainline.' They had to park a block away and walk back to the club's entrance. Before they started back, the guys suggested that the women lock their purses in the trunk of the car, and if they were wearing any expensive jewelry, they should take it off or be very careful with it. Dessie hadn't brought her purse, and the only thing of value that she wore was a string of pearls that Ruthie had given her, and even then, the value was purely sentimental.

Once inside, it didn't appear to be as packed as the cars outside suggested. It couldn't have been more than twenty people inside. The guys pulled two tables together so that no one was left out of the group. Vicki and Fredrick left the table almost immediately to dance to the smooth pulsating rhythm of a popular reggae song. Danny looked at Dessie and she quickly averted her eyes. She wasn't in the mood for dancing. Clive was sitting close to Sharon telling her something that only she could hear. Not trying to be rude any longer, Dessie asked Danny about the club and why there weren't many people inside.

"Dey a pon beach," Danny explained, "dis club a beach front. Big potty a go'won ta night."

"You mean to tell me that we are on the beach right now?" Dessie asked, with an incredible look on her face. Danny nodded his head up and down.

"I've always wanted to walk on the beach at night!" Dessie exclaimed.

"No, no! You mustn't! Beach a not safe in da night!" Danny told her.

"But you just said that there were a lot of people out there!" Dessie reiterated back to him.

"It a safe for dem because dey are all togedder." Dessie thought about what he said for a moment, but got up anyway to follow the rear exit sign.

"Me a must come wid you." Danny announced as he stood up.

"No. I'll be all right," Dessie said confidently, stretching out her arm as if to hold him back, "I have to do this alone." Danny looked dejected as his eyes followed her as she left.

Vicki and Fredrick returned to the table with cold, refreshing coconut water for themselves and the others. "Where's Dessie?" Vicki asked Sharon before she sat down.

"She wanted to take a walk on the beach alone." Sharon said.

"And you let her?" Vicki asked in a panicky way.

"She didn't want anyone with her. Danny offered, but she wouldn't hear of it."

"I know that she's not sleeping well," Debra said. "She almost took my head off when I tried to wake her up earlier." Danny looked real concerned then, and started pacing by the tables; finally saying that he wanted to go and find her.

"She just recently lost someone that she was very close to in her family, and it's taking her through a lot of changes." Debra said, without going into the details of the tragedy. Danny couldn't stand being where he was when he knew that she was feeling bad. He announced to the group that he was going after her and abruptly left in the path that Dessie had taken her leave earlier.

Danny hurried past the revelers with a couple of the women reaching out to drag him into their frenzied dance moves. Danny kept walking on the beach searching for a glimpse of her white dress. When he finally spotted her, he was amazed as to how far she had walked in such a short time. Before he was halfway near her, she stopped and sat down; tucking her feet into the hem of her dress; making a tent for them. As Danny slowly approached her, he stopped at the soft sound of her weeping. He watched a moment; indecisive as to his next move, he called her name as softly as a zephyr, causing her to suddenly jerk her head in his direction.

"What are you doing here?" she asked, harsher than she had intended, "Didn't I say that I wanted to be alone?" she questioned.

"I worry dat some-ting a bodder you. For Who a vex you?"

"What do you mean? What did you say?" Dessie asked, trying to understand him.

"In your con-tree, ya say... some-ting a worry you, no?"

"Oh I understand what you asked now," As she looked up at him in the darkness. Suddenly a new onslaught of tears rendered her speechless. Not knowing what to do, Danny cautiously reached out and bought her close to him as she wept. He held her close to him for a long time. With her head resting on his chest, he was the most comfort she had felt in over a month. When her weeping had ceased, she slid back down to the sand and he followed; never letting her hand go. Once she felt comfortable, she started to tell him about some of the events of the past few weeks. She didn't tell him about the circumstances surrounding Junie Boy's death, but if he were listening as attentively as he appeared, then he would have known what she was talking about. When he knew that it was the right time to speak, he told her the wisdom that had been taught to him. "Me mudder use to tell I; ya con't cry for yesterday. It a gon wid all it trouble. It a only good for de memory. Ya con't know what t'morrow a bring come til it a reach. Ya con only take care of this day trouble. Fe this is all we con andle right now."

"Your mother sounds like a really wise woman. I wish I had met her a year ago before everything got all messed up." Dessie told him.

"Ye would ave ad to meet her five ear gon. She a dead now."

"I'm so sorry to hear that," Dessie told him, "I wouldn't know what to do without my Mama. She helps so many people in so many ways, and I think of how I have hurt her, and I have to make a decision now that will certainly hurt her again. There is no way that I can avoid hurting her if she ever found out my secret."

"When the pickney a push out?"

"What did you just say?" Dessie asked.

"When you a ave baby?"

Shocked by what he had just asked, Dessie was speechless for a few seconds.

"Who told you that?" Dessie demanded to know.

"Me a need nobody fe tell me. Me ave three pickney all ready in Kingston. Me know you a big up." Dessie looked down the front of her dress and she couldn't tell that she was pregnant, but she felt so self-conscious, she wanted to run and hide.

"Fe no worry. Me no tell no one. Where de pickney daddy?" When he inquired about the father, another crying episode ensued. She was finally able to put all the cards on the table, and surprisingly, felt cleansed. When they arose from the sand, two hours had passed. They made their way slowly back down the beach to the club with him protectively holding her hand.

𝒟𝒞

The next few days were fun-filled with a hectic atmosphere in the air. The four friends shopped in the open markets, dined at only native restaurants. The food was excellent and much cheaper than what they had at the resort. In the evening, they knew that the guys were coming to pick them up for a night of clubbing, dancing and some impromptu beach parties. Dessie was starting to really like Daniel, but she was smart enough to know that it was nothing more than a brief interlude to what lay ahead of her.

Danny arranged to get her away from her friends for a long ride to Negril. Dessie fell in love with the area instantly. He added ambience to it by playing the song 'From a little cottage in Negril' by this Reggae Artist

Dessie kept thinking that this was the perfect picture of how she wanted things to be, and she voiced that to Daniel.

"Shhh…" He motioned with a finger to her lips, "t'day is for t'day. Dats de only ting dat matta. Dessie looked into his beautiful brown eyes, and all of his wisdom seemed to shine through. Silent tears flowed after a few moments of losing herself in the glory of him.

"I have a confession to make to you Danny."

"What tis it?"

"That night on the beach…."

"Yes."

"You stepped in and saved my life. I was sitting there thinking about how I've made such a mess of things, and how much better off I would be dead. Had you gotten there ten minutes later, you would have never found me. You've made me see how many lives I would have ended had I gone along with my plans." He looked at her for a moment then pulled her closely to him; lightly brushing her lips with his own as he embraced her.

DC

Later that night, Dessie gathered her three friends together to tell them her news and what she intended to do about It. Once she got them all sitting down, she took the direct approach. "I'm almost three months pregnant." Three mouths opened but not a single sound came forth. Dessie almost fainted from holding her breath so long.

"I thought you said that you went and had an abortion!" Sharon said, still shocked at hearing the news.

"I did go to have it done, but as they were getting me prepped, I heard what sounded like a vacuum, and I fainted. When I came to, the doctor refused to do anything until I had thought about it for at least forty-eight hours. I went home thinking that Ray was just talking out of his head, and that he really did love our baby and me. I knew that any day he was going to come and tell me that he was sorry for trying to force me to get rid of it."

"But Dessie," Sharon started, "what are you going to do about this?"

"I'm going to have it." She said softly.

"Do you know what you're getting into girl?" Vicki said with indignation.

"I know that I can't kill this baby, and this is not some rhetoric from the right to lifers. These are my own convictions. I just can't bring myself to kill this baby."

"Did you ever think about adoption?" asked Debra.

"That to me would be just like going to an abortionist. My child would be dead to me."

"But Dessie," Debra continued, "that would give a child a better chance in life. It would be wanted and loved."

"This child is wanted and loved!" Dessie said strongly, "If not by its father; then most certainly by it's mother!" Dessie was stressed and it was beginning to show.

"I hope that you are not using this as a ploy to hold onto Ray." Vicki added.

"Ray is out of my life!" Dessie convincingly told her friends, "I have to see him one more time, and after that, I hope to never have to see his sorry ass again!"

"Are you certain of that?" Debra asked.

"So help me God! But I need all of ya'll's help."

"For what?" Vicki and Sharon asked in unison.

"I can't live in Westfield any longer, and especially now that I'm about to start showing. I think New York would be a pleasant change. I'm sure I can find a job with my background."

"Citibank is always looking for a slew of people to fill positions." Debra interjected.

"I don't want to burden you guys, but which one of you can I stay with for a while until I can get on my feet?" Vicki and Sharon both said 'me.' Debra told her that since she would be staying with her sister for a couple of months, she really couldn't invite someone else to move in.

"But I can get you around New York." She volunteered.

"And I can help you find a good doctor for the baby and you!" Sharon added excitedly, "this is going to work out great Dessie! Your baby is going to have three wonderful godmothers!" With those words, Dessie let out a relief filled sigh, thanking God for this wonderful blessing.

DC

"I wish for you to stay." Danny whispered into Dessie's ear while hugging her from behind. The beach was deserted, the water calm with the moon appearing to rise up from the sea.

"I bet you say that to all the foreigners."

Dessie teased.

"Only if dey a look like you!" He laughingly breathed into her ear.

"If my circumstances were different, I'll stay right here for the rest of my life." Dessie sadly stated.

"Ye fe try again wid de pickney fodder?"

"I think you just asked me if I was going back to the baby's father, right?" His laughter let her know that she was right.

"Ya fe get good girl! Ya musta be ere for years!"

"How I wish!" Dessie exclaimed, leaning back against his chest.

"You con if ye fe want to." Danny said seriously.

"That wouldn't be fair to you Daniel. I'm carrying another man's baby."

"Fe your seed is me seed too!" he strongly said, "Me a love ya pickney because me a love you!"

"Don't do this to me Daniel! I like you, and maybe more than I should, but I have some obligations that I have to attend to. I have a baby to prepare for in about six months, and that is going to take strength that I don't know if I have. I can only hope that by the time this baby arrives, I've gotten whatever it takes to give it a good life. This child deserves that much." Danny turned her around to face him and crushed his lips to hers. For a moment, they were all that existed.

DC

Danny arrived at the resort an hour early; three hours before their flight departed. Dessie seemed to take the longest to get ready. It wasn't that she didn't want to leave; she had to face Ruth and tell her that she moving away from home. She knew that she was going to tell her that it was because of greater job opportunities, but should Ruthie pry further, she didn't know what she could say to convince her mother that she was making the best decision for herself.

After she was packed and dressed, she went to the veranda and told Danny; who sat staring at the sea, that she was ready to go. He slowly walked into the room and picked up her bags. She could tell that he didn't want to do this by the silent way he moved. She was starting to hurt too. She had feelings for him too, but once she arrived back in Westfield, she would have to be a different person in order to pull off her plan, and she knew that she would only have one shot at it.

When they reached the car, Dessie almost flew into a panic when she looked around and didn't see her friends. "Where are they?" Dessie asked, looking around for her companions.

"Not fe worry, not fe worry!" Danny informed her, "Me get dem nudder taxi."

"Why did you do that?"

"So me ave more time wid you!" Danny said, smiling as if he had pulled off a great feat. Dessie had to smile at his cockiness. As he walked ahead to put her luggage in the car, Dessie noticed that she liked the way he walked; always sure of where he was going. How could any woman not find him attractive and sexy? Once in the car, Dessie instructed Danny on not driving too fast.

"Me no want to drive fast today." He sadly informed her. Dessie studied his face for a few moments. He was so handsome and sad at the same time. She wished that she didn't have to leave.

"Last night me fall in love all over again." Danny told her. Dessie instinctually reached for his free hand and held it tightly; seeking to bring some comfort to an emotionally charged atmosphere. Still holding his hand, Dessie turned her head towards the window so he wouldn't see the misting of her eyes. Each was lost in they're own thoughts. Danny parked in the airport's parking lot, and pulled Dessie close to him; kissing her hungrily with parted lips. She finally pulled away from him before she couldn't. He looked at her for a long moment before getting out of the car to retrieve her bags from its trunk.

Inside the airport, he waited until she had been checked in and was ready to walk to her departure gate. "If ye fe ever need I, dis is me number and me address," Danny said, as he squeezed a slip of paper in her hand. Danny tilted her chin upwards and gently placed his full lips on hers. There was none of the urgency, or the frenzy of the lust filled kiss in the car. This was a kiss of 'understanding.' When they broke their embrace, silence prevailed between the two. Dessie picked up her carry-on and slowly traced his lips with her finger and turned and walked away. When she reached the point where she had to turn, she looked back. He was still standing there. Watching. She gave him a little wave before she disappeared. She looked at the slip of paper in her hand and read the name: Daniel Hewitt. She sighed heavily and slipped it into her purse. 'From a little cottage in Negril...'

"What was taking you two lovebirds so long?" Debra asked Dessie, with a mischievous smile; punctuated with a wink.

"It was nothing like that Debra! Get your mind up out of the gutter!" Dessie teased. "We were just saying goodbye."

"You are so lucky Dess," Vicki stated, "you get off the plane on your first day here, and you fall into the arms of a Jamaican God!"

"If I remember correctly Vicki, it didn't quite happen like that!" Dessie reminded the group.

"Yet and still," Sharon joined in, "you still did better than the rest of us."

"What are you guys talking about?" Dessie said laughing, "Ya'll had a bunch of guys running behind ya'll all the time too!"

"Yeah, but they weren't no Gods!" Debra said in a funny, down kind of way; causing the rest of them to laugh at her.

DC

Dessie and Sharon sat together on the plane, and Dessie revealed her plan to Sharon. She needed Sharon with her for moral support. Sharon tried to get her to change her mind about not telling her mother about the child she was carrying. "What if she finds out Dess? How are you going to explain that?"

"I doubt that that is going to happen. I'm moving away to avoid the possibility of anyone that I know running into me, or seeing me with a child."

"I still think that it would be much easier for you if you told her the truth. You can still leave home. You don't have to stay there. What if something happened and you needed to get back home right away? What are you going to do with the baby?"

"That's why he or she has three wonderful aunts to always look out for baby!"

"You sound a little too confident girl!"

"I wish I felt 'too confident' for what I'm about to do." Dessie said soberly.

"Just exactly what is it you're about to do?" Sharon asked.

"I really don't want to talk about it right now. I still have to work out some of the details. I'll have it all together by the time I'm ready to leave for New York."

"I hope you are not planning on doing something as weird as what you pulled us into the last time." Sharon warned.

"Don't worry! I'll never do anything as crazy as that again.

"You'd better not!" Sharon said, narrowing her eyes at her friend.

Chapter Two

"Baby you look so good!" Ruthie said, embracing Dessie, "I knew that that vacation would do you a whole lotta good! Now you can go back to working and living. I want you to move back here until you get yourself built up!"

"That's what I want to talk to you about Mama," Dessie said softly, "I've made up my mind. I'm going to be moving to New York with my friends." Ruthie seemed to sink to the sofa rather than actually sit on it.

"What are you talking about Dessie Lee? All the family that you know of is right here in South Carolina. We ain't got no kin up in no New York child!" Ruthie said, sounding panicky.

"Mama I'm not going there trying to find any kin. I'm going there to find myself."

"You can find yourself right here if its lost!" Ruthie said.

"Mama you know what I mean! I need to get out and explore my options. Westfield just doesn't do it for me anymore. There are way too many bad memories here for me."

"So you figure that if you move off to this New York, you won't have to remember Westfield; is that it?"

"Mama I need this change. It's for the good of us all. Junie Boy is gone; I'm through with Ray. I need a new start after all that has happened."

"Seems to me that you left out the fact that you have a mother here and a brother that has been trying his best to talk to you since the funeral!"

"Mama you already know how I feel about that, and let's not discuss it anymore. Please?" Dessie said near tears.

"Alright. I won't say anything else, but him and Charlene came here and swore to me that he never knew Desmond was his father."

"Okay Mama, okay!" Dessie said, getting agitated, "I'm not ready to talk to Clanford right now, and I don't know if I ever will!" Ruth Ann looked at her daughter without uttering a sound. She wanted to tell her daughter what the power of forgiveness could do, but to keep pushing at her was only going to drive a wedge between them; pushing them further apart. Plus she felt that she herself was not a prime example of a forgiving soul when you got right down to it. As much as she could forgive Desmond his mistakes, she has not afforded the same to Beulah Mae. What she had to say at Junie Boy's funeral could have waited. She wished that it were she that Beatrice attacked and not Randy fuller.

".... So I'll be moving out at the end of the week."

"What did you say Baby? Mama was thinking about something else."

"I was just telling you that I'll be moving out at the end of the week, and on Sunday I'm leaving for New York."

"So soon Dessie? Christmas is just around the corner. Can't you wait until after the holidays to leave?" Ruthie begged.

"I wish I could Mama," Dessie lied, "but I have a big job interview on Monday and I can't miss that."

"Dessie Lee! Family is always more important than some job!" Ruthie instructed, "Jobs will always be here, but family you only have for a short time."

"I realize that Mama, but this is a one in a lifetime opportunity. If I don't take it now, it may never come again."

"I hope you know what you're doing Dessie Lee! They tells me that all sorts of things go on in that place. Murders and everything!" Ruthie said, trying to scare Dessie into staying in Westfield.

"Who told you all those things Mama?" Dessie asked.

"The television people told me, and they should know cause theys right there!"

"Mama, that doesn't mean that the whole place is bad. From what my friends have told me, they don't live in high crime areas."

"I don't care what your friends told you! I seen right on that television that New York has more crime than anywhere else!"

"That may be true Mama, but New York is a much bigger place with a lot of people in it."

"They look like a bunch of sardines all cramped together walking down the street. I don't know how they could even breathe. I bet you that some of them folks just drop dead on the street cause it ain't enough air to go around!"

"Mama that sounds ridiculous!" Dessie stated, "There is more than enough air to go around for everybody in the world."

"How do you know Dessie Lee? Have you ever been to New York before?"

"No Mama. I haven't, but my friends have lived there practically all of their lives and they are all fine."

"Theys was the lucky ones. You might not be that lucky!"

"Mama I don't think there's anything to worry about, but should something happen, I'll come back here right away."

"Well," Ruthie continued, "you better get you one of those breathing tanks like old Mr. Cooter got. He sit out there on his porch just struggling to breathe. He have to take that old tank with him everywhere he go. One day at the church, he musta run out of air or something. By the time the ambulance got there, he was almost gone. They had to pump a lot of air in him to keep him from dying. He used up all those folk' tanks of air and everything! If somebody else needed some air that day, they was out of luck! Old Cooter used it all up!"

"If they needed more, Mama, I'm sure they would have had no trouble getting it!"

"Yet and still Dessie Lee, you better take two or three of those tanks with you. You might need that good fresh air!"

Dessie was a little relieved when Ruthie said that. It meant that she was getting used to the idea that she would be leaving.

With that out of the way, Dessie needed to close out her apartment. Knowing that she would be breaking the lease, she didn't want to go to the superintendent; so she wrote a brief note stating that due to 'unforeseen' circumstances, she would be vacating the premises.

Dessie posted a couple of signs in the foyer of her building and the one next to it; listing the items that she would be selling off.

Sharon arrived that Thursday to help Dessie pack her belongings. It was time to contact Ray. She called his office three times. On the third try, she told his secretary that since she could not reach him at the office, she would have to show up at his home that evening. Ray called her back five minutes later from his cell phone.

"What is it Dessie? What do you want?" Ray asked gruffly.

"It's so nice to hear your cheery voice Ray." Dessie said sarcastically.

"Look Dessie! I don't have time to play your fucking games!"

"Oh Ray! I'm so sorry to pull you away from whomever you're doing, but this call is strictly business, I'm leaving Westfield in a couple of days, but I wanted you to know that I'm still carrying your baby."

"What the fu...."

"Shhh, Ray. Don't get so worked up!" Dessie said quietly.

"I gave you two thousand dollars to take care of that!" Ray angrily said.

"Oh I know you did, and Jamaica was really nice!"

"That's your problem! I did what I had to do!"

"No! You did what you wanted to do! Neither you or I should ever have the right to take a life!"

"If you feel that you want to have a baby, you go right ahead! I have nothing to do with that!"

"But you did have a lot to do with it!" Dessie said, wavering a little.

"You were fucking me and I don't know how many other brothers at the same time!" Ray shouted into the phone. Dessie felt hurt at his words, but she was not going to be stopped at this stage of the game.

"Whatever you say, Ray! I'm going to keep this baby, and because we both know that you are the father of this child, you need to assume some responsibility for it."

"I'm sorry. I don't know what you are talking about." Ray said, nonchalantly.

"Here's the deal Ray: I need to leave here, and I'm going to have to find a place to live for an undetermined amount of time. I am in need of financial support. I need at least three thousand dollars a month. I could settle this whole matter for a one time payment of one hundred thousand dollars."

"Are you out of your fucking mind?" Ray asked angrily, "I don't have that fucking kind of money lying around!"

"Wait a minute Ray. There's more. This child deserves everything that your other three children have. By the time he or she has turned a year old, I want a diversified portfolio in this child's name with an initial investment of fifty thousand dollars."

"You are one sick bitch Dessie! This shit will never stand up, and I really doubt that that's my baby! You can't prove it!" every time Ray denied that he was the father of her baby he twisted the knife a little bit more.

"Whether you think that I'm lying or not Ray, this is your baby, and DNA can prove it. You do know what DNA is Mr. Morehouse man! Don't you?"

"You dirty bitch! I will kill you before I give you one fucking dime!"

"There, there Ray!" Dessie said as if she were speaking to a little child, "If you don't have this money here by Saturday afternoon, I'll be showing up at your door with some news for your wife."

"You don't have the nerve to do something as stupid as that you bitch!"

"You want to bet on it Ray? Clanford and my mother already know the circumstances, and I will let them in on the fact that you have threatened me!" nervous and wondering what he would do, she hung the phone up and cried until she fell asleep. Sharon shook her awake two hours later; ordering her to get up and eat. Dessie didn't want to, but Sharon wouldn't take no for an answer. Dessie confided to Sharon the things that Ray had said to her, and that she was afraid of him.

"Did he call you back after you hung up?" Sharon asked.

"No. I expected him to, but I'm glad that he didn't. I wouldn't have been able to keep my emotions in check."

"Well, since he didn't call back," Sharon began, "then he's thinking about your offer. You just have to keep your cool." Dessie felt better after confiding in her friend about her feelings on the matter. She had to admit that she was scared, and that she almost gave up when he denied being the father of her child.

"I want to see what he's going to do. If he values his marriage and family, he'll play by the rules."

"What if he doesn't come through?" Sharon asked.

"I haven't thought that far ahead, and I don't want to think about him not doing what I asked!" Dessie explained.

"Would you really confront his wife if he doesn't show up with the money?"

"I don't know. I don't know what I will do." Dessie said, sounding so uncertain.

DC

Dessie and Sharon were awakened the next morning by the doorbell's incessant ringing. Dessie wondered for a moment about who could be visiting at that time of the morning. Suddenly, she remembered that she was selling off the contents of her apartment, and hurriedly grabbed her robe as she rushed to the intercom.

DC

By mid afternoon, Dessie and Sharon were standing at the kitchen counter tallying up a little more than nine hundred dollars.

"You are a natural born saleswoman!" Sharon told her friend.

"No I'm not," Dessie firmly stated, "I needed to get rid of this stuff so that I could move on. What you heard and saw was the act of a desperate woman. I had to sell off everything. Too many memories were associated with every piece of everything that was in here."

"I am glad that you have cleansed yourself of all that, but where are we going to sleep tonight? Better yet, what are we going to sleep on tonight? You sold the bed remember."

"Girl, I already got that covered! I booed a double room at the hotel up at the airport. I'm going to leave the car at my mothers. We'll take a cab to the airport." Dessie explained.

Realizing that they hadn't eaten all day, she decided to go out and get something. Sharon reminded her that she was expecting a call from Ray. Dessie told her that she would be quick about it.

She wished that she had never gone. She was standing at the takeout counter waiting on her order when Clanford and Charlene walked in. He stood for a moment looking at Dessie before walking over and offering a cheerful 'hello.' Dessie was so surprised at seeing him, she couldn't open her mouth. When she didn't speak immediately, a pained expression crossed his face. Dessie reached out; touching his arm. The motion caused him to grasp his sister in a tight embrace. Charlene joined in a second later. Both Clanford and Dessie shed tears. Happiness or remorse, neither knew why. A visibly pregnant Charlene cried at the sight of them. Dessie told them about her plans, and for a moment it seemed to snatch their joy of acceptance of one another. Dessie promised that she would stay in touch with them once she was settled. Dessie specifically asked Clanford to check in on Ruthie often. Charlene and he both vowed that they would. Dessie had a thousand questions for Clanford, but she just didn't have the time to seek out the answers to any of them. They exchanged Christmas greetings and parted company. For the first time since the holiday season began, Dessie actually felt the spirit of it.

When she arrived back at her soon to be former apartment, Sharon told her that Ray had called and wanted her to call him back on his cell phone by three. Dessie looked at her watch. It was already two forty five. Suddenly, she wasn't hungry anymore. She wanted to be beyond the place she was currently at. She wished that Junie Boy was still alive. He always knew what to do. At three o'clock, Dessie picked up her phone and dialed Ray's cell number. He answered instantly. Once he found out that it was she, he stated immediately that he wanted her to meet him privately and alone.

"I'm sorry to disappoint you Ray, but I can't arrange a private meeting with you."

"You want the fucking money don't you?" Ray bellowed into the phone.

"Oh yeah, I need the money to take care of your child, but I don't need to meet you in some secluded spot!" Dessie paused for a moment to give him a chance to think about what he had just asked her. I can have Clanford come with me," Dessie stated.

"That's okay!" Ray quickly said, "I'll come to your place. I'll be there in an hour."

"Just ring the bell. We'll be here," Dessie instructed.

"I was hoping that you would meet me downstairs. I want to see you one last time," Ray said huskily into the phone.

"That won't be possible Ray. I do have guests visiting me." The two guys that were there to break the bed down and remove it were keeping up enough noise to make anyone think that the apartment was packed and the party was in full swing. Ray didn't say anything for a few seconds, and when he did speak, he sounded so defeated.

"I'll be there soon, and you will have to sign an agreement that I had drawn up saying that this payment is a one time offer, and you will never seek another dime from my estate or me. Is that clear?"

"Sure it is; as long as you have it in writing that this child will receive fifty thousand dollars by its first birthday as well." Ray didn't say another word. He clicked his phone off. Dessie didn't allow herself any type of celebration just yet. It was too soon.

As promised, the doorbell rang about an hour later. Dessie went to the intercom, checked who was there and buzzed him in. a few seconds later, Ray tapped on her door. When she opened it she was shocked to see that the man she had been so madly in love with, seemed to age twenty years since the last time she had seen him. She invited him in and proceeded towards the kitchen counter where Sharon was sipping on a cup of tea. Ray reached inside of his coat and brought out two typed copies of the agreement. Dessie briefly read them both over and signed one; giving it to Ray. "I'll let you know the baby's birth date so that you can prepare the final settlement."

"That won't be necessary. I already know when your baby will be born," Ray said in a cold, detached sort of way. He put a manila envelope on the counter and told her to count it.

"I don't think I have to do that Ray. I trust that you did the right thing," Dessie softly said.

"It's more than I can say for you!" Ray angrily said as he turned and hastily walked out of the kitchen. Dessie heard the door to the apartment slam shut, and felt the burn of tears falling from her eyes. Sharon was looking at Dessie in disbelief.

"What are you crying for girl? You got what you asked for didn't you?"

"I never asked for my life to be so messed up!" Dessie said, pounding her fist on the counter.

"Chill out Dess!" Sharon commanded, "You owe your baby more than money! You keep walking around upset all the time; your baby is gonna come here a nervous wreck!" Dessie thought about what Sharon had said. As much as she wanted this baby to have everything, it would mean very little to the child if its mother's mental condition failed to stabilize itself enough to bring a well-adjusted baby into the world.

"I know Sharon," Dessie calmly said, "I just let my emotions get the best of me. Seeing him just irritated me so much! I can't wait to leave here!"

"We'll be gone in the morning, but I think we need to count that money before we do anything else!" Sharon stated with a take-charge attitude. By the time they were finished, neither wanted to see another fifty or hundred dollar bill anytime soon.

"I don't think it's such a good idea to travel with so much money," Sharon said to Dessie.

"You better believe that I won't be just 'carrying' it on my arm in a purse!"

"Don't tell me that you're thinking about packing it with your clothes?" Sharon asked and stated, with a wide-eyed look at her friend.

"No. I won't be doing that," Dessie said, "I'll have a money pouch that I'll be wearing under my sweatshirt. I won't have to go in it for anything, and I'll always be able to feel it around me." Sharon heaved a heavy sigh of relief,

"That's way too much money to lose!"

"Are you ready to leave for the hotel now?" Dessie asked.

"I'm ready. I just have to pack some toiletries that I left in the bathroom."

I'm all set," Dessie stated, "I just have to get over to my mother's to drop off the car and say goodbye. I hope she don't try to keep us there too long." Dessie said as an afterthought.

DC

"Well, I guess this is goodbye for a little while Mama," Dessie said as she hugged Ruthie close to her. Ruthie jumped back and looked at Dessie strangely.

"What wrong with you child? You pregnant or something?" Dessie looked shocked for a moment, then started laughing as Sharon covered her own mouth.

"That's just my pouch Mama!" Dessie said, "I put all my jewelry and important papers in that so I don't lose them."

"That's really smart baby! You make sure them peoples in New York don't do nothing to try and trick you and steal all your stuff from you! You hear me Dessie Lee?"

"Yes Mama. I hear you!" Ruthie hugged both women goodbye; wishing them a safe journey. As the cab pulled off, Dessie turned and looked out the rear window to see a sad Ruthie standing and waving. Dessie discreetly wiped her eyes dry.

Chapter Three

"I have never seen such a big place in all my life!" quipped Dessie. "There must be thousands of people moving around in here!" Dessie said of Kennedy airport, "Where in the world could all of these people be going?"

"A lot of them are just passing through." Sharon explained, as they waited for their luggage to appear on the carousel. Dessie couldn't stop looking around at all the movement going on around them. A considerable amount of time passed before they caught a glimpse of their bags. Sharon had a baggage cart waiting to put their suitcases on.

"I hope my sister is here waiting on us," Sharon worriedly said. "If you are a few minutes late, she takes off."

"Well, it did take us a while to get our luggage." Dessie offered.

"I told her that we might be a little longer depending on what order our luggage was put on the plane."

"If push comes to shove, we can always catch a cab to where we need to go, right?" Dessie asked.

"I hope we don't have to do that," Sharon said, New York cabbies charge way too much. Both of us would have to pay the same amount for going to the same place."

"You mean that even if we are going to the same house, we both have to pay the exact amount?"

"Yep, as unfair as it might seem, it's perfectly legal."

"I guess we won't be taking cabs all that much." Dessie said, resolutely.

By the time they made it to the passenger pick-up area, Sharon could see her sister Diane a few cars away from where they were standing. Sharon hurried Dessie to where the car was so that they wouldn't interrupt the flow of traffic that much. Before Dessie knew it, they were packed in the car and on their way out of the airport. Sharon introduced Dessie to Diane and they were off to their new home in Brooklyn.

DC

Dessie had never seen houses sitting so close together; each one looking the same as the previous one.

"How in the world can ya'll tell if you're at the right place or not?"

"You ever heard of little things called 'numbers?' Sharon sarcastically asked.

"Don't clown me girl! The numbers at home are so big, Ray Charles can see 'em!"

"Well Dorothy, you're not in Kansas anymore!" Diane threw in, as her and Sharon cracked up. Diane was fortunate enough to find a parking spot right in front of the building that was to be Sharon's new home, and for a while, Dessie's too. As soon as she backed into the spot, she popped the trunk so that they could get their luggage out of it.

"Hurry up ladies. I have to get home and spend some quality time with my two lovers. The one that I am married to claims that I'm never home long enough to take care of his needs; so, I'm going to go and take care of my big papa 'needs' if ya'll know what I mean!"

"Don't rub it in Diane!" Sharon scolded, "He gave you a ticket for parking in a handicapped parking space. Remember how much you hated him?"

"Yeah child, I do, but when he showed up at my door with a bunch of roses; the rest is history."

Well girl, you kiss my fine ass brother-in-law!" Sharon instructed her sister.

"We are not that kind of family! I'll give him a handshake from you! I almost had to shoot your trifling-ass classmate over my husband!"

"Who?" Sharon asked.

"That Toni Hitchens!"

"What has that tramp done now?"

"I needed a ride to work to work, and Brandon was in the neighborhood so he stopped and waited in front of the building for me. When I got downstairs, low class ho who has a name brand mattress permanently tattooed across her ass, was leaning over inside of the drivers window. She almost became a statistic! I let her know that I always carry my department issue with me, and that I won't hesitate to use it!"

"And what did Brandon have to say about all of this?"

"You know how Brandon is! He tries to avoid confrontation, but you should have seen what the ho had on; hot pants with fishnet stockings with pant boots, a halter top, bright red lipstick on those oversized lips of hers!"

"Girl I remember those lips! One of our classmates asked her to kiss his yearbook so that he'll never forget those lips!"

"And here it is almost Christmas and the scandalous bitch is still wearing summer clothes!" Sharon said, in a disbelieving tone.

"You should have seen the coat that she had on! It looked like something out of those 1970's movies! It was half pleather and some sort of sad looking fake fur. Just as I was getting into the car, I told her loudly that she should be careful while out working!"

"And what did she have to say when you told her that?" Sharon laughingly asked her sister. Diane stuck her neck out, and brought it back and twisted one corner of her mouth up and said, "Girlll! I always be careful when I go to work!" Sharon, Diane and Dessie all laughed hysterically before Diane got back into the car to leave.

Sharon and Dessie brought their remaining bags up to the second floor apartment.

"This place is huge!" Dessie exclaimed. "It doesn't look that big from the outside, but once in here, wow!" Dessie said as she looked around the spacious living room. "It was real smart of you to pack everything ahead of time and ship it here."

"Honey, I didn't pack anything or ship it either! My job did all this for me. I didn't have to pack anything but my clothes!"

"You must be pretty important to your job."

"I'm in charge of medical delivery services. I see to it that patients who are housebound receive the proper medical services. I set up nurses and aides to go out and work in individual homes. I more or less move people around from day to day."

"That must be pretty interesting," Dessie told her friend.

"It can be a pain in the ass when you're dealing with a bunch of people who don't want to go into certain areas because of this reason or that reason; or someone doesn't show up because they couldn't find a babysitter or something."

"Speaking of babysitters," Dessie started, "is there a good hospital in the area?"

"Yeah, Lutheran is about the best here in Brooklyn. There are others, but Lutheran is the best in my opinion."

"Would they have a listing of ob-gyn doctors?"

"Sure they do! They have a whole network of doctors for everything imaginable."

"Do you think that you can get me to the hospital?"

"I or Diane can. The area surrounding the hospital is her beat."

"Is she a cop?" Dessie asked, looking wide-eyed.

"Yeah. You mean that I didn't tell you that she was a cop?" Dessie moved her head from side to side indicating that she hadn't. Her husband and she are both police officers."

"I thought that she was a security guard."

"They should have a whole lot to talk about when they are not working," Dessie intoned.

"Lets get these bedrooms put together. I have to show up on the job tomorrow, and if I don't get some sleep, I'll be fired before I even get started."

Dessie helped Sharon put her bedroom together, then, the two of them set up the room that Dessie would be using. It was smaller than the one Sharon had, but it was still roomy enough for her.

ⅅℭ

"...You're doing fine Mrs. Cunningham. I estimate that around June first, you'll deliver a healthy child," Doctor Nasir told a nervous Dessie, "even still, I want you to start on the supplements I prescribed right away. What branch of the military did you say your husband was affiliated?"

"He's with the army," Dessie lied.

"And he's in Afghanistan right now?"

"Yes."

"Well hopefully, he'll be home by the time his little one gets here. You may get down and get dressed now," the kindly Indian doctor told her.

"See the receptionist on your way out and she'll set you up for your next visit." Dessie thanked him as he was leaving the examining room. She removed the paper gown and got her own clothes from a hook behind the door. She gathered up her purse and all the booklets he had given her.

When the receptionist gave her the appointment card and called her 'Mrs. Cunningham,' Dessie almost looked behind her to see whom it was that the woman was talking to. When it dawned on her that it was she the woman was speaking to; she quickly tried to recover and begged the woman to please call her 'Dessie.'

Once outside of the doctor's, Dessie began to breathe as if she had been holding her breathe in for a long time. The fact that she had given them a false name unnerved her, but she felt that it was the best way to go. She knew that if Ray had wanted to find her, he could, but there was no way he was going to find her baby. She didn't trust him, and she would do anything in this world to protect her own.

DC

Dessie contacted Vickie soon after her visit with the doctor. She wanted her to investigate the current rates and terms on certificates of deposits at several banks in the area. She knew that fifty thousand dollars weren't a whole lot of money, and that most of would be taken up in living and medical expenses; she still wanted to profit as much as possible from it. After conferring with Vicki, she decided that the only way that she could be sure of having extra income after the baby's birth, would be to take a job of any type, and put forty thousand dollars into four separate certificates of deposits; three long term, and one short term, six month certificate, if she should happen to need it soon after the baby's birth. If not, she could take the money and turn it over into another certificate or, if she felt that she could withstand the risk, a more lucrative investment option. She thanked God for her summers at the bank. The knowledge that she now needed was invaluable. Putting herself on a shoestring budget wasn't easy, but it wasn't that hard either.

The pretty maternity wardrobe that she planned on having was not to be. She shopped at a couple of budget dress shops, and purchased a pair of comfortable shoes and a plain pair of winter boots. Looking behind her to a year earlier, she would have never thought that she would have been in her current situation.

Sometimes, deep into the night, Dessie cried tears of anger and regret. Not wanting the anger to poison her thoughts, she often spent the next day praying and asking for forgiveness. She could never get over how she wouldn't even talk to a guy that she knew had a girlfriend, and here it was, she was having a baby by a married man! She couldn't help thinking that God was punishing her for the choice that she made when she decided to love Ray.

DC

Dessie had seen snow before, but she was no way prepared for what fell her first full month in Brooklyn. It started out with a few flurries in the morning, and by early afternoon, it was a full-blown storm. Dessie spent most of the afternoon looking out of the window and worrying about Sharon; hoping that she would make it home safely.

Seeing all that snow made Dessie wish for home. The more she looked at the snow, the more depressed she became, and soon the tears started. It seemed as if she cried for everything that had gone wrong in her life. She knew that being constantly upset was not healthy for her or the baby. It was a while before she became composed.

Still feeling homesick, she decided to call Ruthie. Just as her mother's phone started to ring, Dessie felt a little fluttering in her stomach. She was so shocked by the sudden movement of the baby, that she dropped the phone and placed her hand in the area where she felt the movement. It happened again. Dessie totally forgot about the phone until she heard Ruthie repeatedly saying 'Hello.' Dessie quickly picked up the phone and sang 'Hello' back into it. It seemed as if it had been an extremely long time since she had genuinely smiled about anything. She wished that she could have shared this moment with her mother, but she told her about the horrific snowstorm instead.

"You don't go out walking in all that snow do you baby?"

"I haven't yet, but I will."

"You better be careful child. If it's as much as you say, you can fall down in it and the folks won't be able to find you."

"Mama, they have folks out working on the streets and sidewalks right now. I've never seen so many people and trucks out working as I have seen today. I heard on the news that they might have to close this whole place down. Traffic is tied up in front of this building. I've been looking at the same cars for the last twenty minutes.

"You just be careful when you go out in it Dessie. Wear two coats so that you stay warm!" Dessie was so happy to just talk to her mother for a few seconds, she would have agreed to wear five.

"What about you finding a job Dessie? Have you found something that you like to do yet?"

"Not yet Mama, I have to work at finding my way around first. I'll probably start looking real soon."

"Do you need any money? I can send you some. I don't want you to have to be a burden on anybody!"

"I have enough money Mama. I saved up money from my job just so that when I wasn't working, I'll have something to live on."

"Okay, but if you need something you let me know." Dessie wished her mother well and promised to call soon.

The snow had her attention once again. It didn't appear as if it was going to stop anytime soon. Dessie wondered if Sharon would make it home at all. She hadn't heard from her since the morning.

Dessie decided to take a short nap since there wasn't anything else to do. The next thing Dessie knew, someone was shaking her awake. She was surprised to see Sharon, but who else would it have been if not her? Came the thought after she had awakened.

"Girl, we had a ball getting home!" Sharon announced, "we walked home, and stopped at every coffee shop on the way. We would have stopped at some bars, but we might not have made it home at all!"

"What time is it?" Dessie yawned out.

"Seven forty five."

"Gosh! That was a long nap I took." She told Sharon about the baby moving inside of her. Sharon said that she was happy for her, but only someone experiencing a pregnancy would understand the joy of the baby's first movement.

"I have to find a job soon Sharon," Dessie said quietly.

"What in the world for? I thought the reason for you getting the money was so that you wouldn't have to go to work for a while."

"When I added up all the expenses and the projected medical costs, providing there are no complications, and the fact that I want to spend more than the average six weeks with the baby, I'll have to start working soon just so I can be home for a while."

I hope you're not talking about a permanent job are you? Cause you wouldn't have enough time in to take an extended leave."

"I'm only looking for something temporary. I'm not interested in benefits or anything like that. Just something to keep me going for at least a couple of months after the baby get here.

"Oh! Something like that is easy to find. There are hundreds of temporary agencies all over the place. We've hired the last five people who work with us from temp services. They had to fulfill their contract obligations with their agencies; after that, they became full-time employees with us."

"How can I find out about the locations of the agencies?" Dessie asked.

"We can pick up a New York Times on Sunday, or we can look in the yellow pages. I can tell you now that most of them are probably going to be in the city."

The City?" Dessie asked, puzzled.

"Yeah, Mid-town Manhattan."

"But how would I get there?" Dessie asked.

"You have to take the F train and get off at 32nd or 42nd streets in Manhattan. It's not that hard to get around. Maybe Saturday or Sunday we can do a trial run, and I can show you how simple it is."

DC

Sharon and Dessie went into the city on Sunday, and it was as easy as Sharon had explained it to her. What Dessie was totally surprised about was that practically all shops and businesses were open. Thinking of Westfield, Dessie knew that on a Sunday, most places were closed. It had only been in recent years since the mall was built, that you could go there and shop on Sundays.

After the mini/instructional tour, Sharon dragged Dessie off to B. Smith's for brunch. Dessie had tried to squirm out of going because she felt that she wasn't dressed up enough to go to such an establishment.

be silly girl! This is Sunday brunch. You come as you are!"

"I just feel so funny about things like that. I don't want people to think less of me by the way I dress."

"Look girl, I met a guy in here one evening who had on a simple sport coat, no tie, and loafers. Every woman that he approached seemed to give him the brush off."

"Maybe he was major ugly or had bad breath or something." Dessie volunteered.

"Nada! Brother was nowhere near to being ugly! All the sisters were looking at this group of brothers wearing the Armani suits and hundred dollar ties looking like they just stepped out of a GQ photo layout." Dessie automatically formed a picture of Ray in her head.

"The brother that couldn't get no play left. When he pulled up in front, the brother was sitting in a black on black brand new BMW with vanity plates that said 'I BANK.' Needless to say, sisters looked beat down!"

"Well at least they still had the GQ crew to choose from," Dessie offered.

"Unh-un! They weren't shopping at the 'Fish market' ,if you catch my drift!"

"So the moral of the story is to not judge a book by its cover," Dessie analyzed.

"And even then, you still don't know what secrets people are covering up-good or bad!" Sharon added.

DC

Dessie and Sharon narrowed their choices down to five temp agencies in the city, and two based in Brooklyn. Dessie went into the city on Monday the way Sharon had shown her. She filled out applications for four of the agencies. She didn't make it to the fifth place because she was too tired. Sharon and she had hurriedly put together a resume that they were certain that no one would be really interested in seeing. It somehow made her feel that it would set her apart from other applicants.

Wherever Dessie went, there were others already ahead of her doing what she was there for. Two of the agencies gave her their brochures so that she could get familiar with their company. One receptionist didn't even look up from what she was doing when Dessie asked for an application. She automatically reached for one and handed it to her. She could have been a serial killer and nobody would have even known in that office.

By the time Dessie arrived back to the apartment, she was so tired from all the walking she had done, she collapsed on the couch. It was easy for her to fall asleep there. It was so comfortable. Dessie heard the phone ringing, but she was so tired, and in such a comfortable position, she decided to let voice mail pick it up and not disturb her rest. It was probably for Sharon anyway Dessie thought to herself. When Sharon came in later, she checked her voice mail and headed to tell Dessie of the message she had retrieved.

"You have to be at work by nine in the morning girl!" she excitedly told her.

"Work? Who…me? Dessie asked, sleepily.

"Yeah, you!" Sharon strongly stated, "The Morgan temp agency left a voice mail that they want you to go to an office on Fifth Avenue in the morning. Here," Sharon said, "listen to it for yourself!" Sharon said as she dialed the access number. Dessie listened to the message, but became a little annoyed when the voice on the other end told her to please dress professionally and went on to tell her in list order what professional attire consisted of.

"They have some nerve calling here telling me how to dress! I could have made up a better list, and then had my mother sit down and make it!"

"Don't take it personally girl! You would be surprised what some folks call professional attire! Party dresses, floor length lounge dresses; you name it! I remember once in Atlanta, we were going out after work; a couple of the girls in the office were already dressed and made up by seven that morning! They were looking at me like *'she going out looking the same way she look at work.'* Ten minutes to five, I went in the ladies room with my bag, hiked my dress up, put a belt around my waist, put on my heels, and make-up complete with lip liner and let my hair down. The little beige jacket that I wore over my dress that day; I turned it into a formal jacket by switching it inside out. It had a black satin lining and no one was the wiser. The other women from the office looked tired to say the least. I looked like I had changed when in fact, I hadn't."

"Well come and help me pick out something to wear tomorrow. I want to look 'professional' you know!" Dessie said with a laugh.

DC

Dessie appeared at the office twenty minutes before she was scheduled. She introduced herself to the receptionist who told her that the office manager was on a call and would be with her shortly. Ten minutes later, an impeccably dressed blond woman appeared out of the inner office and walked over to Dessie with her hand extended. Dessie stood and shook hands with the manager.

"My name is Linda," she said to Dessie, "we are back logged with a lot of our files and paperwork. We need someone who can go into our file room and dedicate the time to putting it back together. There are tons of paperwork, microfilm, newspaper clippings, and hundreds of depositions to file. It's up to you as to where you wish to start. The number one thing that you have to do is to enter on the computer the location of the file. The legal assistant will go to the computer, enter the case number then proceed to the files to retrieve the documents needed. Everything pertaining to the case must be with the file."

Linda opened the door to the file room and Dessie immediately felt intimidated. The room was very large with file cabinets circling the perimeter, and four rows of cabinets running down the length of the room. Just as Linda promised, there were tons of files all over the room. There was one small work desk at the front of the room with a computer taking up most of that. Dessie knew instantly that this was not a day or two job; She had her work cut out for her.

"I've asked the legal assistants to stay out of here for the next two to three days to give you some time to get a system in place. If they need files or depositions, they are to call in and give you enough time to locate the needed file. Also, check the outside of the door when you come in. When the attorneys need something after office hours, they will leave a stick-up on the outside of the door. Whatever file they request its better to get it first thing in the morning. Do you have any questions?"

"Not that I can think of." Dessie replied.

"Well if you do, my extension is right by the phone, and before I forget, your lunch break is from twelve to one. I'll check in on you in a short while."

Dessie looked around at the task before her, and almost changed her mind about taking the assignment, but since quitting wasn't one of the traits that made up her personality, she grabbed a file and set out to find where it belonged. Once she had a place for it, she entered the data onto the computer. It was a criminal matter. She found some colored stickers in the desk drawer and chose the color red to distinguish it from those that were not criminal matters. If the matter was one that involved criminal and civil charges, Dessie copied and made up separate files for both matters. She checked each file to make sure that what was in them belonged. It was sometimes hard not to sit down and read some of the cases. Before Dessie realized it, she had worked through her lunch break. She didn't mind though; she had brought her lunch and didn't have to go out for it.

By the end of the day, Dessie had put a substantial dent in organizing the files. She still had a long ways to go, but she felt that she wasn't going to have any problems completing the task.

After her commute, Dessie walked the short distance to the apartment tired, but satisfied with her day. She couldn't wait to tell Sharon about it. Even before she turned her key in the door, she knew Sharon was not going to be behind it. When Sharon was home, she always had music playing or the television on. Dessie fixed herself a small dinner of soup and a sandwich. She ran herself a hot, soapy bath. Before she got in it, she weighed herself. She was surprised to find that she had put on two more pounds since her visit with Doctor Nasir. Everyone could clearly see that she was pregnant as she looked at her reflection in the mirror.

She tried to picture herself at nine months, but the image could never fully appear in her mind. Finishing her bath, she thought Sharon would have made it home but she hadn't. Dessie decided to turn in for the night. She would have to tell Sharon about her day some other time.

"...Seems like you had a busy day," Sharon said, spreading cream cheese on her bagel.

"It was rather pleasant though. I was able to get so much work done, and still not have to follow someone else's schedule." Dessie intoned.

"That's the kind of job I would love to have. I have to listen to nothing but complaints all day long. The nurses complain, the patients complain. I'd give anything to have just one day a week when nobody has shit to say about anything!" Sharon said, looking upwards as if she were asking God. Dessie had to laugh at her expression.

"So where were you partying at last night?" Dessie jokingly asked her roommate.

"Now, now girl! We don't kiss and tell! But if you really must know, I had a date with this dream of a guy I met a couple of weeks ago. I wasn't gonna give him a minute, but when he showed up in the lobby of my job, I thought that he deserved at least a coffee break! We ended up talking practically all night."

"What's his name?"

"His name is Ben if you really must know, nosey!" Sharon teased.

"He must have been real special for you not to be complaining this morning about not getting your beauty sleep!" Dessie mimicked.

"Watch it girl!" Sharon told her, "Just because I don't look like I went without sleep, nothing can stop me from being a bitch today!"

"What makes that fact different from any other day?" Dessie wisecracked.

"Shut up pregnant!" Sharon threw back.

"Yeah, but… pregnancy only last for nine months… what's your excuse?" Both friends laughed as they headed out the door for their respective commutes. "How long is your assignment for?" Sharon asked.

"Indeterminate," Dessie stated, "I could probably get the whole thing done in two or three weeks, but it can easily stretch into a month or more." By the time they arrived at their subway stop, Sharon was complaining about being tired. "That's what you get for being so beautiful and going out on a date with a stalker!"

"He better not stalk me tonight!" Sharon said firmly, but without conviction. "It's so damn hard to fight off a six two, fine ass brother with all the right moves!"

"You'd better try! Another night without sleep and everybody will have to move out of the building!"

"Forget you Dessie! I'll see you when you get in!" Sharon said as she ran to her bus stop.

Once Dessie was seated on the train, she thought about the fact that Sharon was seeing someone. It seemed so long ago that she was hopelessly in love with Ray. She could have smacked her own self for being so gullible. She had honestly believed that Ray was going to leave his wife and family to be with her. The sadness that she felt every time she thought about the deceit he expertly practiced on her was overwhelming. Had she not cared about her mother, she would have gone public about the affair. She wondered what would have happened. She was sure that his wife would have left him. He might have even lost his job. Right then, she was happy that she hadn't. She wanted him to be around so that she could have her child's future going in the right direction.

For the first time since they'd been back from Jamaica, Dessie thought about Danny, but just as soon as the thought appeared, she let it go. There could never be a future between them. She would never forget the warmness she felt with him. As handsome and sexy as he was, he never once acted stuck-up, or tried to seduce her. In another world and time, she could have seen herself spending the rest of her life with him. When she was with Ray, she always thought about how well he dressed. She knew for a fact that it was nothing for him to wear hundred dollar ties and custom made shoes. On the other hand, Danny dressed simply, but whatever he wore, he made it look good; not it making him look good. Ray wore Armani suits, designer colognes; the best of everything. Too bad that he didn't have anything else to go along with his designer closet. She remembered Danny's kiss, and how it wasn't lust-filled the way Ray's were. The thought of Danny's kiss brought a smile to her lips. She made a mental note to write him soon. She hoped that she hadn't thrown out the slip of paper with his address on it.

When Dessie reached the firm, Linda greeted her as soon as she walked into the door.

"Good morning Dessie!" Linda said with a radiant smile. "I just left a note for you, but since you are here early, I can tell you myself. I have to be out of the office today, and I'm going to need you to fill my shoes."

Dessie was taken aback by Linda's request directive. She was hesitant to take on the job, and stressed her concerns to Linda.

"Don't be silly Dessie! You're the perfect person to fill the position!"

"But I don't have a clue as to how to run an office," Dessie shyly said.

"I've written down everything that you'll need to keep this place running smoothly. It's all on my desk, and that reminds me; you did a wonderful job on those files yesterday. The way you set things up on the computer was simply genius! Whoever looks up a file has to type in their name or the computer doesn't give out the data, or tell the researcher where the file is located. Now we won't have to worry about locating a file. All we need to know is who had it last!" Dessie was pleased with Linda's compliment.

"The last temp girl we had here didn't know what a file was! When I asked her if she knew how to file she told me that the agency didn't tell her that she would have to do nails too! Needless to say, she didn't last very long!" Dessie openly laughed at what Linda told her about the girl. Dessie started to feel comfortable with the impeccably dressed Linda.

"If you should need anything, ask Rayna. She knows where everything is kept, and who's who around here. Gotta run! See you tomorrow!" Linda was gone in a blink. It was almost as if she hadn't been there at all except for the fact that her perfume hung in the air.

Dessie walked over to Linda's desk and studied her instructions. They weren't too hard to follow. The only thing that bothered her was getting all the names right of the attorney's. She had to go to the file room several times to retrieve files that were requested by legal assistants. She would have preferred to be there than to be where she was.

Arriving home that evening, Dessie headed straight for her bed. Sharon was already in hers. Dessie hoped that she wouldn't have another day like she'd had. Just being able to lie down and not be on her feet was absolutely heavenly. She was asleep in ten minutes.

Dessie was happiest working in the file room. She could work as fast or as slow as she liked. Some days were filled with retrieving files, or putting them back in place.

Dessie knew that soon her assignment was going to end, and she looked forward to the respite. She had brought a couple of parenting and motherhood magazines, and she wanted to read them at her leisure. She was taken with the pretty baby clothes, and beautiful nursery designs. But looking at them was all she could do. Painting the walls and changing the décor were not to be. The most that she could fit into the room would be a changing table and a small crib. She tried not to be depressed about her circumstances, but fixing up a baby's room was one of the joys of anticipating the new arrival. It was something both parents did together.

DC

A month and a half after Dessie began the job at Levitts and Howard, the filing system was in place, and very easy to update anytime a new file was added.

On what would be her last day, Linda approached her in the break room and invited her to sit with her.

"You know Dessie, you've done an excellent job here, and I was looking over your resume..."

"I don't recall ever leaving a resume with you," Dessie said blankly.

"No you didn't. I had it faxed to me from your temp agency. We wanted to see what your previous employers had to say about your job performances, and neither of them recalled a Dessie Cunningham..." Dessie's heart felt as if it had dropped into her stomach. She hadn't anticipated anyone actually checking her references for temporary work!

"But they did remember a Dessie Harper, and with a name like that, it had to be you! You've gotten married recently. Congratulations! That's what I wanted to talk to you about today...well, that's included too. I'm getting married in a month, and I'll be leaving for Arizona right after that. The firm wants you to stay on as office manager." Dessie must have been staring with her mouth open because Linda said 'hello' and waved a hand in front of Dessie's face.

"What did you say Linda?" Dessie asked; still surprised, and worried at the same time.

"You don't have to give an answer right away, but we do want to have an idea as to what your intentions are within the next couple of weeks. Not only am I working here everyday, but I also have to run out to Roslyn every evening to help my mom put the finishing touches on my wedding. I tell you! Every time I go for a final fitting of my gown, they have to take it in some more! I'm being run ragged! But I don't have to tell you about it. You've must have gone through the same thing for your wedding." Linda said.

"Oh don't remind me!" Dessie said, with a wide-eyed exaggerated look on her face.

"So, do you think that you might be interested in the position?" Linda asked.

"I have to th... I mean I need to talk it over with my husband first. He's in Afghanistan and I don't know what we'll do once he's back home. Being from the south, he might not want to stay here permanently.

"I understand all too well!" Linda stated, "My hubby to be has joined a law firm in Arizona, and both our families live on Long Island. I know that I'm going to miss them terribly. We hope to start a family soon too."

Dessie hated having to lie the way she did. Now she understood how one lie led into another. What worried her most was the fact that if Ray knew where she was, and the assumed name that she was working under, he could put his hands on her anytime he wanted to.

She had a lot to think about. She hadn't given any serious thought to staying on in New York as a resident. New York is where she wanted to hide. Going back to Westfield with a child was not one of her options either. She decided to wait until she got together with her friends to see what kind of input they had to offer. Dessie wanted to see the references that had been sent to Linda, but she decided not to ask. More than likely, it was from Ray, and the less she thought about him the better.

𝒟𝒞

"…You could ask them if they would be willing to let you have a two month maternity leave," Debra suggested to Dessie, "then if you don't want to return, you can resign."

"But that sounds so cruel and ungrateful!" Dessie stated.

"But you said that you only wanted to work part-time. I don't see how you are going to be able to do that and give the baby as much time as you want," Vicki said.

The four friends had just returned from church services at Brooklyn Tabernacle, and were enjoying a late brunch of fresh fruit and bagels, which Dessie found not to be to her liking. "Don't worry about it girl! Sharon teased, "It's a New York kinda thing!" Dessie rolled her eyes at Sharon and ignored the others laughter.

"But what they are offering you in their employment package, is quite generous to say the least," Vicki said to Dessie. "The salary alone would make me take it without hesitation."

"I would love it!" Debra said loudly.

"Yeah, but you guys are not in the same situation as I'm. If I accept this position; who am I going to get to take care of my baby?"

"I already asked my mother if she would be interested in taking care of a newborn," Sharon stated, and Etta said she'd love to do it since she's retired now, and here's the best part: she can come here and do it so that you won't have to struggle with the baby in the morning," Sharon logically told her.

"Why did you ask her to do it Sharon? I haven't decided to take the position yet."

56

"Well, whatever and whenever you decide, we'll at least have some sort of a plan to play around with, and besides, even if you don't take this particular position, you will have to eventually go back to work. I don't think that you'll get a better set-up than what you have right now."

"You're right Sharon. You're right. All I've been thinking about is spending time with the baby, but nothing past that. I'll let them know by the end of next week what my decision will be," Dessie said, in a somber tone.

"Well since that's all settled, go get the cards Mrs. Cunningham so me and Debra can put a hurting on you and Vicki in spades!" The four friends spent the rest of the afternoon bluffing and cutting on each other.

𝒟𝒞

"...And you are going to be called on to perform some functions that are not in your job description." Dessie raised an eyebrow when Linda said that. "You may not like it, but you can't dictate how others live their lives."

"What do you mean Linda?" Dessie asked. Linda lowered her head and voice as she sat across from Dessie.

"There are a lot of indiscretions that go on around here, and sometimes you will be put in a position where you will have to cover someone else's ass! I mean that you might have to go on shopping trips for the girlfriends or mistresses of some of these guys." A pained expression crossed Dessie's face, and Linda knowingly patted her hand; concerned that what she had told her, upset her badly. "Don't you worry Dessie. It's their lives and they are going to live it the way that they choose to. Last Christmas one of the attorneys here gave me an envelope with twenty thousand dollars in it to purchase a diamond bracelet for his mistress!"

Dessie's head was spinning recalling the sneaking, lying, and hours of passion spent with Ray.

"Why didn't he just write a check or use his credit card?" Dessie asked.

"Don't be silly Dessie!" Linda said, softly laughing "You think they are going to do something like that? Cash is hardly ever traceable! Plus, they wouldn't do anything as stupid as charge something to a credit card or write a check for jewelry or some other expensive item and it isn't for the wife!" Dessie felt so guilty and betrayed at the same time; thinking about her recent past. "Don't look so down Dessie! Just be thankful that our guys aren't like that! The number one commandant around here is; see it, know it, but never say a word about it!" Dessie thanked her for passing the information along to her, but for some odd reason, she felt that what Linda had to tell her, didn't really come from Linda, but from other sources.

" And, also Dessie, these guys are very appreciative around Christmas and other special occasions. I already know that the firm is giving my fiancé and myself a check in the amount of ten thousand dollars for a wedding present."

"Wow!" Dessie exclaimed, "How long have you worked here?"

"As of this past January, five years."

"I'm sure they are going to miss you once you leave."

"And believe it or not, I'm going to miss them too!"

DC

Dessie's first official task at the firm was to put together a going away affair for Linda. A check for four hundred dollars and a note telling her the date and time for the farewell party was on Dessie's desk when she returned from lunch two days after her discussion with Linda.

Dessie didn't have a clue as to where to start. In addition to learning all the ins and outs of her new position, they saddle her with a major task such as this. Once she was settled at her desk, she looked up caterers in the yellow pages. There must have been hundreds listed in Manhattan alone. By the time she had contacted three of them; she started getting frustrated. The company that offered them the best variety of food, came with a price tag of three thousand dollars. The third one that she called hung up the phone on her when she told him how much money she had to spend. To top it all off, one of the legal assistants needed a file for a deposition that was to take place in one hour, and the file could not be found. With her and the assistant both looking, it took almost the entire hour to locate it. With all the other things that she had to do before leaving for the evening, she wasn't able to contact any other caterers. She didn't have a clue as to how she was going to handle this dilemma. She didn't want to ask anyone at the firm. She felt that they would look on her as being incompetent.

When Dessie arrived home, Sharon was already home from her job. Dessie sat on the first piece of furniture she reached. She immediately removed her shoes. Her feet seemed to double in size. Looking at them, she wondered if she would be able to get her shoes back on. Sharon emerged from her bedroom and saw Dessie looking exhausted. "It was one of those days huh girl?"

"'One of those days' just isn't what you would call it! I had to find a lost file for an important deposition, I have to arrange a farewell party for the girl that I'm replacing and the few caterers that I've contacted so far, are way out of my price range, and I don't know what to do next.

"What facility do you plan on using?" Sharon asked.

"It'll be in the break room or the conference room at the firm."

"And what do you plan to serve and for how many people?"

"I was thinking about two entrees; maybe a beef and a chicken dish for about twenty to thirty people."

"How much money do you plan on spending?" Sharon queried.

"They gave me a check for four hundred dollars." When Dessie told her what she had to spend, Sharon understood instantly what the problem was with her plan.

"Girl you will never get what you're looking for for that small amount of money in New York, or anywhere else for that matter!"

"At home, that amount of money would feed two hundred people and a few more besides!"

"That may be true for a Southern church social, but it's not going to fly here in New York! And what's wrong with your feet? They don't look like they belong to you."

"Just one of the conditions of being pregnant." Dessie wryly said.

"I have some scented sea salt. I'll get a warm pan of water and you can sit here and soak them for a while," She said, as went about gathering the needed items.

"That sounds heavenly," Dessie said, and while you're at it, would you cut my nails for me too?" Sharon said something, but Dessie couldn't hear what it was, but knowing Sharon, it had to be something smart.

"...So Sharon, what am I going to do about this party?" Dessie asked, as Sharon lathered her feet with moisturizing lotion. "That feels so good girl! You need to do this every evening!" Sharon stopped what she was doing and gave Dessie that 'you're plucking my nerves' look. "You still haven't told me what I should do about this farewell thing."

"That's really simple. They are not interested in having a dinner. It's just a little get together for friends."

"How do you know that?"

"By the amount of money that they gave you. All they are looking for is a big cold cut platter; preferably of turkey, roast beef-medium rare, a few cheeses like Brie, and maybe a couple of domestic brands. You get some coleslaw, onion dip with assorted crackers, and make sure you have a lot of coffee, sandwich rolls, mayo and at least three types of mustard."

"Girl, You really know this stuff don't you? But tell me, how am I supposed get all this stuff to the office?" A puzzled Dessie asked.

"You don't have to worry about that either. I have a couple of friends who own a deli not far from where you work at. I'll give you their number and you can call them and they will deliver the spread right to the office. Problem solved!"

"But what am I going to do for dessert and alcohol?" Dessie asked, feeling flustered again.

"You won't need to order any alcohol. All you need to have in the way of that is a few bottles of celebratory champagne. If they want something stronger than that, they'll go to their offices for it. And as far as dessert goes, you can have a cheesecake designed any way you like at that bakery we bought the cookies at. Just make sure that you give them a couple of days notice."

"You are a life saver girl! I was so upset about having to do this thing to the point that I was making myself sick!"

"Don't worry about thanking me. You just don't know 'New York style' the way I do!" Dessie pulled the pillow from behind her and threw it at Sharon."

DC

The informal gathering was a huge success. Linda couldn't stop thanking Dessie enough for the well set-up break room. "You have to tell me what you're having! Is it a boy or a girl? I want to send you a nice gift for the baby."

"I don't know what the sex is yet. When my doctor asked if I wanted to know, I told him that I would rather be surprised."

"I think that that is so traditional! Technology has taken away the element of surprise. I think I'll do the same thing when we start planning for a family. When is the baby due?"

"My doctor says that I should deliver on June seventh, but I'm getting so big lately, the baby may get here earlier than that."

"That's two months from now," Linda observed, "you don't have that long to go."

"Thank God for that!" Exclaimed Dessie. "I don't think I can take the stress of having to go further than my due date."

"I'm sure that you are going to be fine and a great mother too!"

By seven forty-five, most of the guests had already departed. A few of the lawyers were standing around casually talking to each other. Dessie wished they would leave, or at least go into an office or the conference room.

She was sitting at her desk, exhausted and looking at her swollen feet in her shoes when the office cleaners came in. she was elated. Now she could clean up the break room and be on her way home. She asked the two Spanish-speaking men to accompany her to the break room to put a few tables back in place. Once inside, Dessie pointed to the buffet table that had left over cheese, meat and rolls; an assortment of delicacies.

"If you guys would like something to eat, please feel free to take as much of it as you like." The attorney from the firm that was speaking with the others that she assumed were also attorneys, came over to where she was standing with the two men.

"Mrs. Cunningham, my name is Attorney Mortson, and it is not your duty to feed anyone not associated with this law firm. In the future, please stick to your job description. The food that is left over is to be thrown out! Is that clear?" Dessie was so appalled at his comments and instructions, she could barely get a quiet 'yes' out of her mouth. The two guys looked embarrassed as well as the other two guests. They wished Mortson a good evening and left quickly. Dessie gathered up her things and left the building as well.

Dessie was furious with what had taken place. Normally she was afraid of the annoying homeless people on the subway and their relentless pursuit of coins from the passengers. One such person approached Dessie and she went off.

"Why don't you go and get a fuckin job! Everybody else around here works! Why in the hell don't you? You or nobody else better not ask me for shit!" Nobody else went near her. She got off at her stop just as angry as she had got on.

Sharon could tell something was wrong by the way Dessie came into the apartment. She could hear her every step, and Dessie always kept the noise way down. When Sharon saw Dessie, her suspicions were confirmed.

"What happened, Dessie?" Sharon asked, concerned. For a few seconds Dessie couldn't speak. When she could all the anger and confusion came tumbling out of her like a flood. Dessie told her the whole sad story as to what had her in knots. "Something must be wrong with him," Sharon stated. "A person just doesn't act like that over a few measly crumbs! Has he ever said anything to you that would make him appear to be racist?"

"No, never. He has never really spoken to me past saying 'good morning.' I don't have a lot of contact with the attorneys at the firm. Most of my time is spent with the legal assistants."

"Why don't you ask them about this attorney? Maybe they have observed the same behavior he exhibited with you," Sharon suggested.

"I don't know about that," Dessie said, calmer than she had been a few moments earlier. "They work closely with the lawyers, and they might think that I'm trying to build a case or something."

"Did he say anything that would indicate racism?"

"No he didn't, but it was obvious what he was doing."

"Ten different people could view that same scene and every one of them would come up with a different interpretation. The burden of proof would rest on you." Dessie sighed heavily.

"I wish I had Linda's phone number. I would definitely call and ask her about this guy."

"Why don't you wait until tomorrow when you get to the office and look it up?" Dessie agreed. She was drained from the day's activities, and sitting there worrying about the incident wouldn't solve it, or make it go away. Sharon fixed them both a cup of herbal tea, and they talked until it was time to go to bed.

When Dessie arrived at work the next morning, she looked in the Rolodex on the receptionist's desk for Linda's number. Once she had copied it down, she placed the slip of paper under the blotter of her desk. She would call later; during her lunch hour. Her routine didn't deviate from what she normally did everyday. When Harry Mortson showed up at the office, he gave his customary 'good morning' and moved on to his office. His behavior was normal. He didn't appear angry or annoyed like he was the night before.

Dessie stayed busy most of the morning; passing off typing assignments to the secretary and the receptionist. They didn't like it, but it was the rule, should things start to get backed up, they were to help out. Dessie would have liked to do it herself, but she needed to be able to talk to Linda without interruptions. When Dessie got Linda on the phone, she wasn't expecting to hear what Linda told her.

"Last year on his wedding anniversary, his wife Tillie decided to take the train in from Glen Cove, that's out on Long Island, to take Harry to lunch to celebrate. It was a big deal to Tillie. She never came into the city without Harry. They adored each other. They never could have children, so they were the center of each other's lives. Some Puerto Rican kids from the Bronx stole a car. They were only thirteen and fourteen, and they drove to the city at the same time Tillie was crossing the street to get to the firm. She died on the spot. That was bad enough, but Harry was leaving the building while all the commotion was going on, and he figured that it was nothing more than a fender bender and kept walking. When he came back from lunch, the police were waiting on him. Tillie was buried the next morning. All business at the firm was put on hold for twenty-four hours. It was two months before Harry could return to the office. Everybody loved Tillie and Harry. He blamed himself for everything. Tillie had been begging him for the last two or three years to retire. She had wanted to move to Florida to be near her sister, but Harry kept putting her off telling her that he would retire the following year. Of course the owner of the car did not have any insurance, and nothing at all happened to the kid who hit her. The juvenile court system let the kid go with a warning. It tore poor Harry apart. He will never be the same. Try to cut him some slack Dessie. He's a hurt man, and he wasn't attacking you. He did a lot of good in this world."

"I feel so bad now Linda. I understand what it feels like to lose someone that you love at the hands of someone else. I'm going to pray a special prayer for Mr. Mortson." Dessie thanked Linda for the information. She suddenly realized that she had not cornered the market on grief.

When Dessie got ready to leave the office, she placed a call to the apartment and left a message on the answering machine that she was going to do some shopping for a few maternity outfits. Now that she was working full-time at the firm, she needed to look the part. The few dresses that she had weren't going to be enough to carry her to the end of her pregnancy.

By the time she finished shopping, it was almost eight o'clock. Before she left the store, she slipped off her shoes and put on a pair of corduroy slippers that she kept with her when her feet became swollen or tired. When she arrived at the station, her train was just pulling in. She hurried to get a seat; smiling at her own self for looking like a bag lady. She grabbed the first available seat that she saw and settled in for the ride home. As the train started to move, Dessie looked out on the platform where she noticed two well-dressed guys holding briefcases talking. When she looked into the face of the guy looking at the train, her heart felt like it would stop beating. He looked like Darryl. When his gaze continued to follow the train, she knew that it had to be him. *"What in the hell is he doing here in New York?"* She thought to herself.

All the memories of so long ago came back to torment her. She would never forget how humiliated she felt standing at his dorm room door practically begging him to take her virginity.

So caught up in the memory, she almost missed her stop. She couldn't wait to get into the apartment. She needed to tell someone what she had just experienced, but there was no one to tell. Sharon had left a note on the table saying that Ben and she had gone to the movies, and not to wait up for her. Dessie knew that that meant she wouldn't be home until sometime after midnight. Why should she stay home on a Friday night? She's not the one walking around with a huge seven-month belly! Dessie started to feel depressed. The events of the last couple of days had taxed her spirit to the point where she just wanted to curl up in bed and not have to think about anything. Who ever said that pregnancy was a woman's crown, had to be out of their minds!

Chapter Four

Dessie had wanted to tell Sharon that she thought that she had seen Darryl, but after thinking about it, she decided that it served no useful purpose and tried not to think about it again.

Early on the first Saturday in April, Sharon woke up an extremely tired Dessie who had had a rough time finding a comfortable position to sleep in, and had tossed and turned throughout the night.

"What's wrong with you Dessie?" Sharon asked.

"Nothing is wrong. I was just thinking."

"You know how to do that?" Sharon asked in a fake excited, exaggerated way.

"Sharon, why are you bothering me on Saturday morning, and let's not forget, *early?*"

"We got to go shopping!"

"For what?" Dessie asked, almost annoyed.

"Shopping for the baby silly!"

"But I won't be having the baby for almost another two months!"

"So after you have this baby, you gonna get up and go shopping for him or her? That's not the way you do it! I have Ben's car. Get up and get ready while I fix us some breakfast. We have forty-five minutes to get outta here!" Dessie pulled her bulk up and prepared to take a shower.

Dessie felt as if they had hit every store, every outlet there was in New York before ending at Kids R Us. Dessie was so miserable and tired; she wanted to pluck out Sharon's eyelashes one by one! "Can we go home now Sharon?" Dessie begged, "I don't think I can stand up for another second!"

"We need to get some diapers and tee shirts for the baby too, or did you forget that babies don't get up and go sit on the toilet when they have to 'go'?"

"Don't be sarcastic Sharon! You know that I know babies don't get up and go to no toilet!" Dessie said, showing her annoyance.

"Well, this all could have been easily done if you would have let the doctor tell you whether you were having a boy or a girl."

"I don't want to know until its here!" Dessie said.

"That's why we had so much trouble finding stuff," Sharon stated, "blue for boys, pink for girls."

"Now wait a minute Sharon!" Dessie said, tiredly, "If it's a girl or boy, I'm not going to be dressing him or her in all blue, or all pink all the time anyway!"

"It's not just the color that I'm talking about. You see more and more infant clothes designated sex appropriate. You can tell just by going in the stores and they have sections for boys and girls who are not even born yet! There's no more middle of the road!"

"With all the stuff I bought today, at your insistence may I add, my baby will be well dressed no matter what it is! Can we go home now? I'm starving and I need to rest," Dessie moaned.

"Yeah, we can go now," Sharon said, picking up the diapers and tee shirts. "Let me call Ben and tell him he can come and pick up his car. By the time we reach home, he can already be on his way. Sharon spoke to Ben briefly as they made their way to the car.

Once they had arrived at the apartment, there were no open spaces to park in front of the building; so Sharon let Dessie out in front as she eyed a parking space across the street. Dessie started up the stairs with several bags. She would come back down and help Sharon with the rest.

Dessie put her key in the lock and opened the door to loud shouts of 'surprise!' Dessie looked around, startled from the shouts. The living room was filled with mostly people that she didn't know. The entire room was decorated on a stork theme of blue, pink and yellow. A frilly, white bassinet sat in the middle of the floor in front of a chair decorated for her. A tall light-skinned man took the bags out of her hands while Vicki led her to the chair. Her main thought at the time was who were all these people? She knew Debra, Vicki and Diane, but the others; she had no idea. As if reading her mind, folks started coming up and introducing themselves to her.

After meeting everyone, a woman wearing an apron appeared in the doorway leading from the kitchen and announced that the buffet was ready. When Dessie saw her, she knew that the lady had to be Sharon's mother, Etta. Sharon was the exact replica of her. The two could have easily passed for sisters.

Dessie was so amazed by the scene in the living room, she was the last person to go into the kitchen. She was swept away by the act of total generosity; she didn't feel that she deserved all of this special attention. When she could reach her, she gave Sharon a tight hug; thanking her over and over for this wonderful surprise. Sharon saw the tears about to begin, and grabbed some napkins from the kitchen counter and handed them to her. "Don't cry girl! This is a happy moment!"

"That's why I'm crying! I'm so damn happy!"

"Well you can save those tears for later! I want you to meet my guy! Ben!" Sharon called out. The guy that had taken her bags when she came into the apartment turned and looked in their direction and started walking towards them. "Ben this is Dessie, Dessie meet Ben. They shook hands and exchanged pleasantries. When he walked away, Dessie told Sharon what she thought of him.

"He is so fine girl! No wonder you kept him hid!"

"He's not into pregnant women; so I ain't worried!"

"Pregnancy doesn't last forever!" Dessie flippantly told her.

"Just wait until your behind go into labor! We'll see how interested you are in a man then Miss Thang!" Dessie and Sharon giggled over their private joke as they heaped food onto plates. Dessie ate as if it was the first time she had ever been hungry.

By the time the party started to wind down, so did Dessie. She thanked the remaining guests for their gifts, and excused herself to go and lie down. Dessie slept peacefully for the first time in months.

Dessie was three days past her due date, and beginning to feel anxious. She had gone into the office for the last time the previous Friday. Her stomach looked and felt like it was hanging rather low. Her back had been hurting her since very early that morning. She followed Dr. Nasir's instructions about lying with a couple of pillows to support her back. That didn't make her feel any better. In fact, every position she switched to, only made her hurt more.

By the time Sharon arrived home from work, Dessie was up pacing the floor; complaining of her back pain. "Have you tried calling your doctor?" Sharon inquired.

"No. He's only going to tell me to put pillows behind me so that I can get some rest, and its just not working today!"

"You should get on the phone and let him know what's going on." Dessie reluctantly gave in and called her doctor's office. She told the nurse who answered the phone what was happening. After a brief period of silence, she put the phone down and went into the bathroom and returned with the digital thermometer in her mouth. When it beeped, she read it to the nurse, "ninety-nine point five" followed by a few seconds of silence from Dessie.

"No. My water has not broken as far as I..." at that very moment, Dessie felt a warm trickle down her leg, "I think it just broke!" Dessie blurted into the phone. Within the next few seconds, Dessie was off the phone and telling Sharon that she was in labor and her water had just broke. "I need to get to the hospital right now!"

"How do you want to get there?" her friend asked, "cab, ambulance, or do you want me to see if Ben or my sister is available?"

"Whichever is quickest!" Dessie said, as she made her way to the bedroom where she slept to get her pre-packed overnight case, and to change her damp underwear.

Sharon called Diane's number, but no one answered there, so she called Ben's and told him what was happening. He told her that he would be there in about fifteen minutes, then called her back and asked what her address was! When Dessie came back into the living room, she found Sharon laughing so hard she had to laugh too.

"Ben is so funny, Sharon managed to say, "I told him what was up, and that we needed a ride and he said he'll be right here. Then he calls me back to ask for our address! He's only been here a *thousand* times! Now I know that if I decide to marry him, I'd better not depend on him to get me to the hospital to have our baby!" The two laughed some more. The doorbell sounded; their cue to come downstairs.

Dessie was pushed to a labor room after she had registered into the hospital. Sharon stayed with her.

After being examined, Dessie was told that she had a ways to go since she hadn't dilated that much. She begged to see Doctor Nasir, but was told that he was in the delivery room and would see her as soon as he could get away. A monitor was placed on her abdomen.

"I guess Ben and I won't be hanging out tonight." Sharon announced.

"Why don't you go ahead Sharon? I'm going to be here for a while. Don't change your plans because of me!"

"Don't be silly girl! You don't have anyone here to be with you, and Ben and I can go out anytime. I'll go tell him that he can leave and I'll get in touch with him later."

"Thanks so much Sharon. Even though I've read everything I could lay my hands on about giving birth, it's still a little scary."

"Don't worry about it Dess. I'll be with you, and if we need reinforcements, I can always call in Debra and Vicki," Sharon said as she left the room to go tell Ben that he could leave.

When Doctor Nasir finally came in, he examined Dessie, and told her that the baby was large, and that he more than likely would have to perform an episiotomy on her prior to delivery. Dessie told him that she didn't want it, but he convinced her that it would be easier to repair a man-made cut than a rip.

In between slight contractions, Dessie rested and even slept a bit. Sharon was soon on Dessie's schedule. She dozed off and on as well. After one particular sharp contraction, Dessie awoke sweating. They were coming closer together now. From their estimation, she had been in labor for at least thirteen hours. It was seven p.m. Dr. Nasir told her that it was going to take longer because she had only reached three centimeters. She had wanted to cry because of the discomfort. Sharon was right; she didn't want to have anything to do with another man!

Dozing off was out of the question now. The contractions were getting stronger and closer together. She was just about to tell Sharon that she thought that she had seen Darryl a couple of months back, but a severe contraction hit her and all she could think about was getting away from the pain. She bore down to try and ride with it, but a nurse appeared and cautioned her about pushing too soon. Dr. Nasir came back and had Sharon leave the room for a few minutes while he performed the episiotomy. "Don't worry Mrs. Cunningham," Dr. Nasir began, "Sometimes giving birth for the first time takes longer, but everything is moving along right on schedule. You will be going to the delivery room soon."

'Soon' wasn't getting there very fast! She wanted to scream that she needed something for pain, but she didn't want the baby to have to bear the slightest risk of drugs entering its bloodstream. She had to endure this without pain medication.

A nurse came in to check on her a half hour later, and told her that she was ready to go to the delivery room. She was fully dilated. The nurse asked Sharon if she would be going to the delivery room with Dessie. Sharon looked at Dessie and saw that she was in so much pain and decided right then that she was going to go in with her.

The nurse had a scrub suit outside on the cart. She gave it to Sharon; instructing her where to go to get ready, and how to get to the delivery room.

When Sharon arrived at the delivery room, she found everyone in position. She went to the head of the table so that Dessie would know that she was there. Dessie grabbed Sharon's hand just as another contraction hit her. She tried not to scream out as she pushed, but she couldn't help it. The pain was too intense. She felt like giving up. She didn't want to have this baby naturally afterall. "Please Dr. Nasir! Just put me to sleep!" Sharon's face had lost all of its color as she tried to comfort her friend; who was holding her hand so tightly that it had became numb.

"You're doing fine Mrs. Cunningham!" Dr. Nasir said, assuring Sharon if not Dessie. When she had to push, Sharon held onto her as if she were drowning. A nurse announced that her blood pressure had risen considerably. Dr. Nasir told her to stop pushing as he checked her pressure himself. He decided right then that he would have to use forceps to expedite the delivery. Just as he was asking for them, Dessie experienced three severe, earth-shaking pains, and the baby's head appeared with its mouth open but no sound. A nurse immediately suctioned out its mouth and nose as the rest of the baby was born. Now you could hear the high-pitched wail of a newborn.

"It's a boy Mrs. Cunningham!" Dr. Nasir announced. "You have a big fine son! He's perfect!" A nurse hurried and wrapped him in a heated blanket and placed him in Dessie's arms, just beneath her breast. Dessie looked at her son, then up at her friend. Tears were streaming down Sharon's cheeks. Her son was no longer crying as he tried to fit his whole fist into his mouth. He was so beautiful. He didn't have much hair, and his coloring was splotchy, but Dessie couldn't see that. His newborn loveliness captivated her. When the nurse reached to take the baby, Dessie started to protest, but the nurse told her that it was necessary to weigh the baby, get him ID'ed, and perform some other needed functions. Dr. Nasir was busy working on Dessie. Sharon went to call Vicki and Debra to share the joyous news.

DC

Iren James Cunningham was born on June 10th at 12:04 a.m. weighing in at 9lbs 6oz. Dessie had been pondering for the last two months what she would name her baby. She knew for sure that if she had a son, the middle name would be James in honor of her beloved cousin, Junie Boy. Had she given birth to a daughter, she would have named her Irene Ruth. She loved the name she had chosen. It said strength and sensitivity all at once.

She had decided early in her pregnancy that she would breast feed the baby, and when he was brought to her, being exhausted didn't matter; this was her son, and tired or not, she would always be there for him.

His coloring had changed to a light tan. His little wisp of hair was jet black. The second that the attendant placed him in her arms to nurse, he yawned, stretched, opened his eyes for a second and began to cry. The nurse showed Dessie how to get him to suckle.

"You may have to do this two, or three times until he gets used to it." Dessie didn't think that she would have to use the 'flicking' technique on Iren again from the way he hungrily suckled at her nipple. As he got full, he dozed off and was sleeping soundly in minutes. Dessie placed him in the hospital basinet and laid down herself. She watched him sleep until she too drifted off. Upon awakening, the baby had been taken back to the nursery and a large bouquet of spring flowers were on the nightstand next to the bed. A nurse appeared almost instantly and told her that she would help her with her bath. Dessie wasn't prepared for the pain that came with getting out of the bed. The nurse noticed the painful expression on her face and went to assist her. "I'll wait until later to take a bath," Dessie told her.

"You have to get up now Mrs. Cunningham," the nurse stated, "If you don't the pain will only become worse." With the nurse's assistance, Dessie struggled to stand and took small, painful steps to the bathroom. "It gets easier as you start to move around," the petite young nurse told her. Dessie didn't believe her for one second! She felt as if her body had been ripped apart. She wanted pain medication, and she wanted it then.

Along with the medication and warm bath, the pain seemed to subside a bit. The nurse helped her dress and suggested that they walk down to the nursery. Iren was right in the first row of infants. He was sleeping soundly. Dessie stared and tapped on the glass to try and wake him.

"Don't worry Mrs. Cunningham. He'll be awake shortly. It's almost time for his next feeding. Let me help you back to your room. I have to show you how to use the breast pump so that your little guy can be bottle fed too."

𝒟𝒞

Sharon, Ben and Vicki came to see Dessie that evening. She had just finished feeding Iren when a light tap on her room door indicated that she had visitors. All three of her visitors were in awe of her precious son. Each held him, and was soon taken over by the magic that only a newborn could create. Ben held him for the longest. He didn't want to give him back to Dessie to put to bed.

"When are we going to do the 'baby thing' honey?" Ben asked Sharon with a sly wink.

"After what I witnessed last night, I don't think I'll ever want to be a mother!" Sharon said, sounding as if her mind was already made up.

"Having a baby can't be all that bad!" Ben said. All three women looked at him in a way that said if he says another word, they were all going to jump him at once!

"Why don't you go and try to pass something out of your butt weighing nine pounds and twenty two inches long!" Sharon laughingly suggested to him.

"Don't forget the six ounces girl!" Dessie threw in, as they laughed. They were about to 'tag team' Ben, when the visiting hours were over announcement came on.

"Ya'll go on ahead Vicki," Sharon said, "I have to speak to Dessie privately for a second." As soon as the door was closed, Sharon told Dessie that her mother had called, but Dessie wasn't prepared for what Sharon told her next.

"She said that last night, she felt that her child needed her, and she couldn't help her. She said that around midnight, she sat straight up in the bed as if she had never gone to sleep at all!" Dessie was surprised, but not shocked. It was the same way she had felt earlier when she sensed that Iren was crying, and no one but she could comfort him. A few minutes later, a nurse was wheeling a crying, red-faced Iren into her room. She now understood what a strong thing the maternal bond was.

"I told her that you were still at work at the law office, and I was over my mother's. She said that she didn't want you out in the streets late at night. I told her that my sister, who is a police officer, and myself, go and pick you up from work whenever you have to work late. She was glad about that, and you could hear the relief in her voice."

"Thanks for covering for me Sharon. I don't know what I'll do without you."

"You'd do just fine without me!" Sharon said, as she headed for the door, "I told her that your office was handling a very big case, and you would probably have to work late a few more days. She wants you to call her when you have a few moments to spare. You'll be home in another day or two; so I wouldn't worry about not getting right back to her."

"I'll call her as soon as I get home, and thanks again Sharon." Dessie felt comfortable with the knowledge that all was working out well.

Chapter Five

Dessie had just finished giving Iren his bath and his evening feeding. She swore that he had gained at least another pound in the few days since they had been home.

Bath time was as relaxing for Dessie as she assumed it was for Iren. He fussed a little at first, but calmed down as she swathed him with warm, soapy water. Soon, he had a balled fist up to his tiny mouth, and sleepy eyes; threatening to close before his bath was finished. Once dry and comfortably clothed, Dessie sat in the Hitchcock rocker that the firm had sent as a baby gift, and read and rocked her sleepy infant quietly to sleep.

DC

"What do you mean that she is living there now Mama?"

"That's what I said Dessie Lee! I couldn't leave my own niece out on the streets like that!"

"But Mama, where is Aunt Beatrice? How come Patrice isn't living with her?"

"Child you know as well as I do that Beatrice ain't never had no time for her chilluns. She only worried about what Wesley is doing. That new car that she brought with some of that insurance money, Wesley done wrapped it around a telephone pole. They says that it happened down by the old railroad tracks four thirty in the morning.

Some of them old bums that live under those bridges said they saw a woman stagger out of the car and run the other way. The police had to go to Bea's house to question her about why this man was driving her car and didn't have no driving license; said they both had to meet court sometime this month. And to top it all off, Patrice met some woman at the store one day, and the woman gave her a job babysitting her three chilluns while she work the late night shift at some nursing home in Anderson.

She got up in the middle of the night to check on the chillun, and tripped over the woman's glass coffee table; broke it and had to go to the hospital that same day that Wesley tore up that car. Bea was cussing up a storm when the hospital called and told her that the girl was there and needed somebody to come and pick her up. The child had to have twelve stitches in her head. Bea told them people at the hospital to put her in a cab and send her home. Bea shoulda got up and went and got that child. The reason Bea put her outta the house..."

"Aunt Beatrice put her out Mama?" Dessie asked, shocked by this new revelation.

"Yeah, she sho nuff did! Patrice went to Bea and told her that the woman she work for, told her that she had to pay for her coffee table, and she wanted three hundred dollars right then and there! Patrice asked Bea for the money, and Bea told her that she better work for free until she worked it off. Patrice told her that she offered to do that, but the woman wanted the money right away for her table. Bea gave it to her after the woman called and told her she needed her table replaced. Bea jumped on Patrice and told her she needed to go and stay with the woman since she paid for the woman's table. Now if that was Wesley, she would've just *gave* him the money. But her only daughter, she put her out on the streets. The lord sho ain't pleased with her!"

"But how did Patrice happen to come live with you mama?"

"Reverend C.L. and Charlene was coming from the church late one night and saw the child walking on the street with practically no clothes on..."

"With no clothes on?" Dessie asked, in a shocked tone.

"Well, the little bit that she did have on, wasn't enough to cover up a little bitty child let alone a big grown gal like Patrice! I called Beatrice and asked her why she threw that child out the house with them little pieces of clothes on. She start hollering and cussing that she had on clothes when she left out of the house!"

"What did she have on when she got to your house Mama?"

"Some little short pants that was way too short for her! Some little thing wrapped around her breast that she called a halt or something like that."

"A halter top?" Dessie asked.

"Yeah, that's what she called it, and she had on some patent leather looking high heels that she could barely walk in. I don't know how long she was out there walking around, but when she got here, she ain't sat down no longer than ten minutes and she was out cold. The poor child was so tired, I couldn't even wake her up to tell her to go and get in the bed. I just put a blanket on her and left her on the sofa."

"Well Mama, is Aunt Beatrice paying you to keep Patrice there?"

"Child no! Patrice pay her own way! She still babysitting every night. Sometimes when the woman has to work double, I may not see Patrice for two or three days. Every week she give me fifty to eighty dollars. She real good about paying her own way. I just wish she wouldn't spend all her money on that make-up stuff."

"That's okay Mama. A lot of young women like to wear make-up."

"But they know how to put it on! Patrice came out of the bathroom one evening and nearly scared me to death! Child, I was almost screaming at the top of my lungs! I thought a murderer done broke in the house! Reminded me of that crazy movie where the clowns was going out killing people. I told her *that* night that she needed to go back in that bathroom and wash all that old mess off her face 'fore she scare them little children to death! She be looking like a clown all the time. You can tell Bea ain't never took up no time with this child. I can't blame it on Patrice. She don't know how to do a lot of things cause her mama just ain't never had the time to teach her nothing, and I don't wear no more than a little lipstick when I go out, so I can't show her how to put all that other mess on."

"I wouldn't worry about it Mama. She'll realize that it doesn't look right, and she'll tone it down herself."

"I hope so child. I really hope so," Ruthie said with a tired sigh. Dessie felt so bad for her mother. She wished that she could be there. In one sense, she was glad that Patrice was there, but she could feel that Patrice was headed down a path filled with nothing but trouble.

"Do you need anything to help you out Mama, food or money?"

"Naw Child. Mama don't need nothing. Reverend C.L. or Charlene comes by here everyday, and if I need anything, they are more than willing to get it for me, or take me where I have to go. I want you to take care of yourself, and give the lord some of your time," Ruthie reminded her daughter.

"I do Mama, but promise me that if you need some help, you'll call me right away okay?"

"I will Dessie Lee, and I want you to take care of yourself."

"Yes Mama. I will. I'll call back soon to see how you're doing. Take care and I love you."

Dessie had her suspicions concerning Patrice's 'babysitting' job, but she didn't say anything about it to her mother because she would probably put the girl back out on the streets, or become severely paranoid concerning her safety.

DC

Four weeks into her maternity leave, Sharon called Dessie from work and told her not to leave until she got there. Dessie had gotten into the habit of taking Iren out for a walk in the early evening before giving him a bath and putting him to bed. She didn't have the faintest idea of what it was that Sharon wanted to tell her. She had been spending so much time with Ben lately, he probably finally proposed to her.

Whatever it was, it certainly had her very excited. Dessie smiled at the thought of her friend getting married.

"Girlll, you will never guess who I talked with today!" Sharon told a curious Dessie. "I won't play a guessing game with you, 'cause I know you'll never guess who!"

"Who was it?" Dessie asked.

"Darryl"

"Darryl who?" Dessie asked, suddenly puzzled.

"Darryl Matthews! Your old flame from our Virginia days!"

"Oh my God, It was him!" Now Sharon was puzzled and asked Dessie to explain what she meant.

"A couple of months ago, I was coming home from Linda's farewell party when I thought that I'd seen Darryl. He wasn't wearing his glasses; so I wasn't sure if it was really him. But the way he looked at me..." Dessie's voice trailed off as she thought about the first guy she fashioned herself to be in love with.

"Why didn't you tell me that you saw him?"

"I wasn't absolutely sure that it was him, and I had intended to tell you about it, but something came up and I forgot all about it. Where did you see him?"

"I didn't see him," Sharon stated, sipping on a glass of juice. "He called the office today to arrange for nursing services for his wife."

"His wife?" Dessie asked, surprised.

"Yeah. He's married, and his wife is very sick, and from what he has told me, she might not have too long to live."

"What's wrong with her?"

"She has ovarian cancer, and from what Darryl told me, she's in the late stages of it."

"Shouldn't she be in a hospital or something?"

"Hospital care is not what she needs. She's terminally ill, and all that they are going to do right now is medicate her and keep her comfortable. She can receive that type of care right at home. I suggested to him that he try hospice care, but he was totally against that; saying he promised her that he would never leave her in a place like that." As if reading Dessie's mind, Sharon gave her the answer to the question forming in her head.

"No they don't have any children. He married her knowing that she had cancer. She was diagnosed just before their wedding." Dessie felt pity for Darryl.

"Do you know how long they've been married?" Dessie asked.

"I didn't ask, but I don't think that it's been that long; maybe a year or two."

Dessie sat and thought about how tough a time he must be having watching his wife slowly die in front of him. She didn't know what she would do if she was in a similar situation.

"He asked about you."

"What did you say Sharon? I was thinking about something else."

"I said, Darryl asked was I still in touch with you." Dessie jumped up thinking that Sharon had told him that they were roommates.

"You didn't tell him I was here did you?"

"Calm down Dessie! I didn't tell him anything other than the fact that we speak on occasion! But you need to know that there is a possibility that you two might accidentally bump into each other sometime in the future. He's working at a law firm in the city, and that alone could put you two together."

"God I hope not!" Dessie moaned, "I don't want to run into him."

"He's living not too far from here. He and his wife live in Brooklyn Heights. That's about a twenty minute ride from here. It's a relatively exclusive part of Brooklyn; mostly homeowners."

The news was disturbing to Dessie that Darryl lived so close to where she was currently living. She could withstand the possibility of running into him, but she didn't want him to see her looking so 'matronly.'

Sharon had been bugging her since the second week after Iren's birth to join her Saturday morning exercise group to get back into shape, but Dessie declined because she didn't want to leave the baby with anyone even for a couple of hours. She regretted not taking Sharon up on her offer, but she was going to join her now, even if she had to bring the baby with her. Dessie got up to go to the window to look out on the street below, but she did it as if she was spying and not wanting to be seen.

"Girl, what are you doing?" Sharon asked, observing her friends secretive behavior.

"Just looking out the window, Why?"

"Well, you sneaked up on it as if Darryl would be standing down there looking up to see you."

"He Could!" Dessie shot back.

"Impossible! I never told him where I lived!"

"Well you know his address don't you?" Dessie asked defensively.

"It's my job to know his address! How else am I going to get the services that he'll need to him?"

"I wasn't thinking about it that way," Dessie intoned, "I saw it as if you were talking to an old friend, and the two of you exchanged addresses and phone numbers."

"You got a lot to learn girl! A person working the type of job that I do, don't ever give out their personal phone numbers to clients. That phone would be ringing twenty-four seven!"

"I guess that does make a lot of sense. I'm just scared of running into him."

"What in the world for? Sharon asked. What you and he had ended way back in college. He moved on and so did you. You never have to say another word to him! You have got to stop living in that perfect coloring book world of yours!"

"What is that supposed to mean?" Dessie asked, mildly annoyed.

"It means that it's alright to color outside the lines. Experience life as it is. Every situation that we find ourselves in is not going to kill us. Sometimes we think it will, but we go to sleep, and we wake up the next day and we deal with whatever obstacles there are in our way, blocking us from getting from point 'A' to point 'B'.

"I guess you're right," Dessie slowly said.

"I know I'm right! Now go get that boy up so we can walk up to Junior's and get a slice of that fabulous cheesecake!"

"You can eat all the cheesecake you want! I'll have a frozen yogurt. Anymore weight on these hips, and I'll be the poster child for overeaters anonymous!"

DC

Dessie was sitting at her desk earlier than usual on her first day back from her maternity leave. She knew that she was going to have a lot of work to catch up on; so she was prepared to come to work early for the next few weeks.

She thought about Iren every minute that she had been away from him. She could still hear his pitiful crying; as if he knew that she was leaving him. She wanted to turn around and go back into the apartment as soon as she closed the door, and she would have done it too if not for the plans that she had for her son and for herself. It was going to cost her some money, and since a top-paying job had been dropped on her, she could see a lot clearer as to how she was going to survive over the next few years. The one thing that she was undecided about; was how she could manage raising a child alone, and seek an advanced degree at the same time.

Dessie had bought a picture of Iren to work to place on her desk. Looking at her beautiful son, she wondered if Ray ever took a moment to think about the child he had fathered. He was so beautiful, how could anyone not want to see him? She picked up the phone to call Etta to see how he was doing. Etta picked up the phone after the first ring.

"Is everything okay miss Etta?"

"Is something supposed to be wrong? And my name

is 'Etta!' you Southern girls are so big on manners! Relax honey! I was just sitting here working on my crossword puzzle, and waiting on you to call."

"Me to call?" Dessie quizzed.

"Yep. All you young mother's are the same! So worried that something is going to happen to the baby as soon as they get on the job, but sugar has been fed, changed and put back to bed. He's doing fine, but you gonna be out of a job if every time you think of him, you jump on the phone to call and check on him! Now get your behind back to work!"

"Okay Mis..I mean '*Etta!*' I'll see you when I get home."

Dessie felt comfortable after talking to Etta. She relaxed and put her mind on the matters at hand. The first thing that she had to do was to secure tickets for one of the attorneys to fly out to Vegas for a five-day conference. What she didn't seem to grasp was why his wife was going to be joining him, and why would she be flying from Texas when they lived in Sag Harbor? It puzzled her all morning until his wife called the office to speak to her husband who had just left for a business lunch. "Please tell George to not forget to stop the newspapers before he leaves for his conference. If he needs to reach me, I'll be at the house in Westport until he gets back. Thank you!"

Dessie had the answer to the complex travel arrangements. She hated what she had just heard, and she wondered how many times she was the other Mrs. 'Whoever' when she and Ray went out of town. She wished that she could go back in time and change the course her life was on. Now, she was determined to never be taken for the fool she had been in the past.

DC

"Come on girl! Keep up!" Sharon yelled to the rear of her. "We got to get your energy level up!" Dessie wanted to knock Sharon on her shapely ass! She was out of shape, but she thought that she would break into it lightly. She wasn't sure if she could handle this kind of workout twice a week. Sharon lapped her for the second time, and she stopped trying to keep up with her and just started walking the track; determined to show Sharon something even if it was only walking.

When they went into the sauna, Sharon was telling Dessie that she and Ben were going to go to the Will Downing concert.

"Don't tell me that! You know how much I love Will Downing!"

"You want me to have Ben get you a ticket?"

Dessie thought about it for a few seconds.

"No. That's alright. You and Ben go ahead and enjoy it. Two's company and three is a crowd," Dessie said, trying to sound wise.

"That's silly! If you want to go, you should! Ben and I spend lots of time alone! Sharing our evening with you is no problem. Plus, I know Will's wife Audrey; we went to school together."

"I'll rather wait until I'm in better shape before I start hanging out," Dessie said, laughing at her own goal. She really did want to go, but she felt so guilty about leaving Iren when she went to work, that she tried to spend all her down time with him. She could tell that he knew who she was by the way he cooed and gurgled at her touch.

She loved Etta and how she instantly made him her 'grandson.' Usually by the time Dessie exited the bathroom, Etta was already fussing over Iren and getting him up. "Com'on now. Gram's baby got to get up!" It made Dessie so comfortable knowing that Iren too had someone that he could call grandma. It hurt her deeply that it wasn't going to be her own mother that he would be calling his grandmother.

𝒟𝒞

Late in November, Dessie once again had her mind on returning to school. She wanted an advanced degree, and she wanted to be well into it before Iren got much older. She had been toying with the idea of taking a class at Long Island University. The Brooklyn campus was very accessible. She was still undecided as to what she actually wanted it in, but becoming a lawyer was one of the fields she was considering.

She decided that she would go over to the college to speak to an advisor once she left work.

Before she left the office, Dessie called Etta to let her know that she would be at least an hour late.

"That's okay honey, but your mother called and she needs to talk with you. She told me that your aunt was in the hospital very, very sick." Dessie was silent as she took in the information.

"Dessie?"

"Yes Etta?"

"Your mother told me that they don't think that she is going to make it."

"I'll be right there Etta!" Dessie said, hanging up the phone quickly. Once Dessie reached the subway for the ride home, she realized that she had never told Etta that she hadn't told her mother that she was having a baby. In the face of this though, her having a baby was a minor thing. Yet and still, she didn't want Ruthie to find out now with what she was facing at home.

When she reached the apartment, Etta was feeding Iren his baby food; which he seemed intent on spitting out. "Did my mother say or ask anything else when she called Etta?"

"Honey, why don't you come on out and ask does she know about the baby?" Dessie's heart seemed to land in her stomach. Without moving, Etta looked at her seriously before breaking into a wide grin. "Of course she doesn't know!" Etta told her, "and no, Sharon didn't tell me! I *told* her and she had to admit it." Dessie breathed a pent-up sigh of relief.

"Etta, did she say how long my Aunt Beatrice has been in the hospital?"

"No, she didn't tell me anything other than she's very, very sick."

"Etta would you hold Iren for me for a little while so that I can talk to my mother?"

"Sure Honey! Go on in your room and close the door. I'll be here with him until you get done."

"Thanks so much Etta. I'll try not to be long."

"Take your time. That's your mother and you only get one of those!" Dessie hurried into her room, closing the door after her. Dessie hastily dialed the number, praying that Ruthie was home. After three rings, Dessie was about to hang up just as she heard Ruthie's voice.

"Hello?"

"Hello, Mama?"

"Yes, it's me Dessie Lee."

"What in the world is happening there?" Dessie asked, hoping for the best.

"Dessie," Ruthie said sadly, "Bea is in the hospital real sick. The doctors done already told us that she only have a slim chance on making it."

"What's wrong with her Mama?"

"Drinking! All that drinking has finally caught up to her. Her liver is barely working."

"What are they doing for her Mama?"

"I guess they are doing everything they can to help her, but the doctors already said it's only so much that they can do."

"Where has Patrice and the twins been while all this has been going on with Aunt Beatrice." Dessie asked.

"I haven't seen Patrice since Saturday when she went to her job. I don't know why that woman that she works for don't hardly ever give that child a night off! Plus, she always working some double; so poor Patrice don't even get a chance to come home for two or three days at a time!"

"Mama, I think Patrice needs to find a regular job with regular hours." Dessie didn't want to tell Ruthie that she really doubted that Patrice was baby-sitting at all.

"Brent told me the other day, when I called to wake him up for school, that Patrice was there and she had woke him up so he wouldn't be late."

"Wesley must be up at the hospital all the time Mama."

"No he ain't! That man went up there the first night and ain't been back no more!" You could feel the anger in Ruthie's voice.

"Maybe he's depressed Mama, and don't want to see her that way."

"From what Clanford and Charlene say, he ain't depressed at all. They see him on the streets everyday dressed to kill, and being with his hoodlum friends drinking and carrying on like the whole world is one big party."

"Some people handle stress differently Mama."

"We sure do know that *he* handle it differently!"

"Don't let it bother you Mama. All of us here are going to be praying for Aunt Beatrice and the family."

"That's real good Baby, but when is you gonna come home?"

"I want to come now Mama, but you have to work a year before you get any vacation time, and that won't happen until the New Year comes in."

"I'll keep you posted on how Bea is doing, and I want you to call home more often than you do. I forget half the things I want to tell you, but let me tell you this before I forget it again; Beulah Mae was standing on the top step at the church when one of Hattie Mae's bad tail chillun's bumped into her and knocked her down the stairs and broke her leg. It took six big men to lift her up! I said to myself, that's the first time I've ever seen six mens carrying somebody that ain't even dead yet!" Dessie didn't mean to laugh, but picturing what Ruthie had just told her, caused her to giggle.

"Mama, I got to go now, but I'll call you back in a few days." Dessie promised.

"Okay Honey. Bye now." Dessie hung up the phone and took a few moments to pray for her aunt.

When Dessie went back into the living room, Etta asked her what the problem was. "My mother said that due to her drinking, her liver has been seriously damaged."

"Cirrhosis." Etta said.

"Sir what, Etta?" Dessie asked.

"Cirrhosis... when a person has drank so much, so often," Etta said as she gathered up her stuff to leave, "they're liver sometimes stop working, or barely works. If the doctors can bring her back, she can never take another drink if she wants to continue living." Dessie thanked Etta for being there for her when she needed her most.

"Honey don't be thanking me for a few minutes that I would have spent standing in the subway anyway!" Etta said as she left.

DC

A few days later, Dessie kept her promise and called Ruthie back. "How's everything going Mama?"

"Pretty much the same Dessie. Patrice came in this morning, and I asked her was she going to go and see her mama, and she told me that she was going after she took her a little nap. That was eight o'clock this morning, and she ain't got up yet! She said that she have to go to work tonight too. Seems to me that that woman would let her have some time off seeing that her mama is sick and all."

"That's gonna have to be up to Patrice Mama. I don't feel that's it's her job that's keeping her from going to see her mother. I don't think Aunt Beatrice and Patrice have ever had too much in common. I'll bet you anything that right about now, Patrice doesn't care what happens to her mother. Look how Aunt Beatrice treated her over the years. Would you care about somebody that had beaten you until you could barely walk?" Ruthie sighed after she thought about what Dessie had said.

"I suppose you right. Beatrice did seem to suck the life right out of Patrice. She only cared about those twins. Junie Boy and Patrice were treated like dogs. I guess whatever love she had for them, James, Junie Boy and Patrice's daddy, must have beat it outta her. Lord, my poor sister needed all kinda help a long time ago!" Ruthie cried, "I just didn't know how to get it to her!"

"Mama don't do that to yourself!" Dessie said, forcefully. "Aunt Beatrice needed to go and seek out help for herself, and she wouldn't!

She was a battered woman and she didn't know how to help herself; so her children suffered because of the abuse she had experienced. It had nothing to do with you! You were always there for them. She was the one that lost all hope. Please Mama, don't blame yourself."

Dessie believed that she had gotten through to Ruthie because Ruthie had stopped crying. "I want you to take it easy Mama. If things go from bad to worse, it'll be you and me to tend to everything. We've got to keep praying that she makes it. Promise me Mama that that is what we'll do."

"I promise Dessie." Ruthie couldn't see the tears streaming down Dessie's cheeks.

Dessie had gained additional growth as a mother. She was no longer concerned about just herself, but about everyone else around her. She worried about the time coming when Iren would want to know the whereabouts of his dad. She didn't want to tell him that he was dead, and she didn't want to tell him that his father had not wanted him; that sounded so cold and unfeeling; even if it was the truth. Trying to work the truth into every scenario that she could imagine, she had to put it out of her head; thinking to herself that she had at least a couple of years to come up with some type of way to work the truth into the explanation. She just didn't want him to find out the way Clanford and she had found out that they were brother and sister.

DC

By their fourth visit to the health club, Dessie was finally able to keep up with Sharon on the track. She was winded by the time they finished, but her improved performance made her want to celebrate. She felt good, and she knew that she looked it too! Sharon also had noted the change in Dessie. "Girl, I better sneak over here and get in an extra workout before you have me looking like the ugly stepsister!" Sharon jokingly exclaimed.

"You're full of it Sharon! You know damn well that I'm no ways near you in anything! You have a gorgeous figure, beauty and brains, and not to mention a fabulous guy to go along with it!"

"You can have the same if you want it!" Sharon said. "Stop hiding in the house all the time. Getting burned once doesn't mean that you should stay away from fires! Every man you meet is not going to be like that jerk! You just have to learn the difference."

"Maybe I do, but the last time I checked, fire still burnt!"

"You know what I mean girl!" Sharon said, rolling her eyes at Dessie.

"Hah ha! You look so funny when you do that Sharon!"

"Well I'm not trying to be funny! That baby of yours is almost six months old, and you haven't gone out once since he's been born! You look great, but why bother working on yourself if all you gonna do is hide in the house?"

"I don't hide in the house! I go to church and I go to work."

"Dessie stop playing dumb! You know exactly what I'm saying! You have not gone out on a date since you moved here!"

"For my first six months here, nobody would have asked me out on a date anyway!"

"I see plenty of guys looking at you, but you won't even give them a smile!"

"Perhaps they look like ax murderers to me!"

"Don't be silly! Contrary to what you might have heard, the streets of New York are not overcrowded with inmates of Rikers Island!"

"I understand what you are saying Sharon. I'm just not ready to start looking for anyone to spend my spare time with. Since Iren came, I have a whole new agenda to tend to. I don't hardly plan on staying single until he grows up! I know marriage may not be in the picture, but I'm still a romantic individual. My priorities are just different right now."

"We'll give you a little time, and let you do your thing, and then we are going to drag you off to all the hot spots in the City until you find someone to have fun with, and looking like you do, it'll happen quickly!"

Dessie and Sharon left the health club and went to shop for a couple of business suits. Dessie ended up buying one suit and a dress. She could wear the jacket with the dress, so she didn't spend any more money than she had to. Not that she couldn't afford to. She had always been thrifty and out of habit, she never splurged.

DC

"How's everything going Mama?" As the holidays approached, Dessie called Ruthie frequently, knowing that she was depressed with all that was taking place.

"Everything is pretty much the same since we last talked. Bea isn't responding to the treatments, but the doctor say her condition ain't got no worse."

"That sounds good Mama. She's holding her own."

"Yeah, that's what the doctor say. I just keep praying everyday."

"Well how's Patrice and the twins been getting on Mama?"

"They's alright. That Boyce won't even go to school lessen somebody make him, and usually nobody do. I swear that boy is just like his daddy! Brent is more like his mama side."

"What about Patrice Mama? How is she doing?"

"Well, last week she didn't come here at all; said she had to work straight through the week. But looks like she got a whole set of clothes at that woman's house. She don't never come home in the same clothes she left in. But she come in here with money. That lady she work for pays her good for watching her kids. Back in my day, you only got two or three dollars for keeping folks kids; five if you were lucky."

"I hope you are saving some of that money Mama."

"Now child, you know that I don't spend nothing on anything I don't need! Since Patrice been living here, every dime she done gave me done went into the bank. She don't eat much cause she ain't never here; plus I have my sewing, and this year I have seven Holland Hills girls to make gowns for. Ever since Tasha won that year, more and more of them are starting to come my way." Dessie heard Iren start to whimper and cut the conversation short.

"I have to go now Mama. I have some papers to get ready for work tomorrow. I'll call again soon. Bye now." Iren was teething and she knew that he was feeling miserable, and only holding and rocking him would sort of calm him down.

DC

Dessie made up her mind to undertake coursework towards a graduate degree. She went to Long Island University's Graduate center where she looked over the graduate course listings. She saw a couple of courses that she was interested in, and decided that she would make a decision over the next couple of days. She knew that it was going to be expensive, but with her salary, and all the money that she had saved, plus what Ray had given her, she wouldn't go broke trying to finance her plans.

Speaking with a counselor, she decided on Business Law to be the first course she would do. It was held one night a week, Wednesday, from seven to ten. She was glad of that. Had it been on a Monday, she doubted if she would have been up to going after a task-filled weekend. Sharon promised her that she would keep Iren for her while she attended classes. They had a daycare center for young children, but the stipulation was that they had to be walking, talking and toilet trained. Dessie didn't want to leave him with total strangers anyway.

DC

Christmas Eve brought in a flurry of excitement. New York's social scene was in high gear. Many law firms hosted their own Christmas parties. Some were so big and elaborate, they had to be hosted at a few hotels and restaurants. It was Dessie's job to pass on personal invitations that came in for various members of the firm. Even more importantly, she had to make sure that when the entire firm had been invited, to type memos so that everyone knew 'where,' 'what,' and 'when.'

Because of her prompt attention to matters relating to other law firms seeking information on files, depositions, wills, and any other matters pertaining to the other firms, she received a few invitations to attend some of the festivities herself. She knew that she wouldn't be going to any of them. Iren was her life now, but she also knew that one day, he was not going to be enough. She missed being in love, but she was also afraid of it. She started many times to analyze it to find out if it was love that she had felt. Most times, she could say 'yes,' but other times, she only saw the sex that held Ray to her. She didn't like the feeling.

The one thing that she couldn't analyze was Ray's feelings. He had told her, but she felt that she would never know why he practiced the deceit that he so cleverly devised. It made her cry; not for him, but for the fool she had been. She wished that June would hurry up and come so that she would never have to worry about seeing him again. *"Take care of your baby, and you will never have to worry about me again."* Dessie said, practicing it to make sure that he would know that she meant it. Or, the alternative, and she knew that he didn't want that!

Dessie sent Ruthie a pair of Diamond earrings. She told her in the card that she sent along with them, that she should wear them to church. Ruthie would never buy herself something so extravagant. It was so hard to make her spend money on herself. She deserved it, but always saw something else, or somebody else that needed the attention. Dessie would buy things for her mother and rip up the sales slip so that Ruthie couldn't take it back to the store.

Dessie picked out stuffed animals for Iren; new clothes, and a new mobile for his crib. She knew that he wouldn't know the difference, but she wrapped each gift in colorful wrapping paper. She placed them around their small tree. She bought Etta a bright green goose down quilt, and Sharon a beautiful gold bracelet. Dessie didn't want anything for herself. She was just happy that she could show her family of friends and her mother, that she loved them, and appreciated all the help and support that they had shown her and Iren. Being where she was at, was present enough.

On Christmas Eve, the firm closed at twelve noon. Dessie was so happy that she would get away from all the shoppers and the packed subways. Even a little extra time spent with her beautiful son was a gift.

Iren's hair had started growing out the last couple of months, and his big beautiful curls were so soft, Dessie couldn't resist twirling them with her fingers.

When Dessie opened the door to the apartment, she had expected to see Etta sitting in the recliner, but instead, Sharon was sitting there; looking glum and redeyed.

"What's wrong Sharon? Is everything okay?" A new batch of tears started. Dessie reached for the box of Kleenex and took some out and gave them to Sharon.

"Darryl's wife died this morning," Sharon said.

"I didn't know that you that you knew her," Dessie replied, stunned.

"I didn't know her. I've never even met her, but I talked to her practically everyday. Darryl is heartbroken. The nurse called him and told him to come home. She died in his arms five minutes after he got there. This is something that happens everyday in my line of work, but this time I feel such a loss. I can just imagine what he's going through right now. He was really shook up when I spoke to him."

Dessie told Sharon that she was going to put on some tea, and come right back. Her thoughts were of Darryl and his pain. Even though their break-up was not amicable, she still felt sorry for him. Dessie brought the tea back to the living room on a tray and placed it on the coffee table between Sharon and herself. "Has he planned a funeral service yet?" Dessie asked.

"There won't be one. It was her wish to be cremated. A memorial service will be held when Darryl feels up to it."

"Are you saying that there will be no body at the service?" Dessie asked, incredulous.

"Yes. It's what she wanted." Dessie had never heard of such a thing before. At home, only funerals were held as far as she knew; with the body present.

"Will you be attending the service?" Dessie asked her friend.

"I don't think I ever planned on that. It's not like she was a personal friend of mine. We simply had a patient/provider relationship that was relaxed enough to border on friendship. I know that Darryl wasn't taking it too well this morning. He asked me to call his office and have the secretary notify family and acquaintances."

"Well, at least he's not going to be in this alone. I'm sure some of his relatives and hers are probably with him right now," Dessie said with more hope in her voice than she intended.

"I'm pretty sure that they are," agreed Sharon. Iren started crying and Dessie went to attend to his needs. After he was fed and changed, Dessie played with him; letting him jump in her lap until he was contented. Dessie took him in the living room that was now dark except for the tree that went from blue to red to green and back to blue. Sharon was playing a Christmas CD of various artists as she prepared a bath for herself. She and Ben were planning on going out for the evening. She had told him that she had wanted to stay home, but he wouldn't take no for an answer. Sharon took dress after dress from her closet; putting it back for some imagined flaw. She finally settled on a gray suede skirt set with matching boots and turtleneck sweater. Dessie suddenly felt very alone and terribly sad. She wished that she too were getting ready to go out for a romantic night on the town. She looked into Iren's sleeping face, and changed her mind. She wouldn't trade him for all the romantic evenings in the world. Dessie put her beautiful sleeping son to bed.

Chapter Six

"Hello Mama!" Dessie said cheerily.

"How you doing Baby?"

"I'm doing fine Mama. How is Aunt Beatrice getting along now Mama?"

"Oh Dessie! Let me tell you what the doctor said! He thinks Beatrice is going to make it! It's still a rough road ahead of her, he said, but he thinks that she is going to pull through!"

"That's wonderful Mama! I know the kids must be especially happy about that."

"Well, the twins seem to be. Patrice hasn't said anything about it one way or the other."

"What are you planning to do for the holiday Mama?" Dessie asked as if she didn't know.

"Clanford, Charlene and the children will be here, and Bea's children and Wesley are 'sposed to be here too. Brent told me that I shouldn't spect to see Wesley cause he gonna be cooking rocks or something foolish like that. Why in the world would anybody want to cook rocks?" Dessie knew what it meant, but she didn't want to tell Ruthie what it was.

"Oh! I won't! Clanford and Charlene don't like being around him anyway. He ain't been to see Bea in four or five weeks. Where you gonna be spending tomorrow at?" Ruthie asked.

"We are going to Debra's for dinner

"Who?"

"Debra Mama. Remember the friend that came with Sharon to Junie Boy's Funeral?"

"Oh yeah, now I remember. Well, ya'll have a good time, and give them my love for me."

"I will Mama. Take care and don't work too hard. I'll call you soon."

DC

Sharon and Dessie both had their hair cut and styled right after Christmas. Sharon had hers done because she and Ben were planning a New Years Eve get away to a cozy bed and breakfast in Connecticut.

Dessie had hers cut for another reason. She was going to start school in a couple of weeks, and she didn't need the hassle of having to worry about her hair when her time was going to be limited with the amount of studying she was about to undertake. She hoped that she was prepared for it. It seemed like years since she'd been in school.

On the evening of her first class, Dessie mistakenly went into the wrong lecture hall and spent fifteen minutes listening to a lecture on European Economics. When she finally located the correct class, she felt all eyes on her. She quickly took a seat in the rear of the lecture hall. Two hours later, the professor allowed the class a twenty minute break. Dessie stayed seated. She didn't smoke or drink coffee; so she called home to see how Iren was taking her absence.

"Girl, You better pay attention to your class! Iren is doing fine. I just fed him and he's back in bed. Don't worry about him! If there's a problem, believe me, you'll be the first to know!" Dessie hung up her cellular relieved that all was going well.

Two weeks into the course, Dessie joined a Brooklyn study group hosted by a very attractive brother named Stephen. The group met at Stephen's apartment every Friday at seven. It was usually over by eight thirty. Before joining, Dessie checked with Stephen to see if it was okay to bring Iren along with her if she was unable to find a sitter. It wasn't a problem.

"I keep my two year old every other weekend. I know how it is when you don't have a babysitter. I can't tell you how many times my friends have called me to go out on a Friday or Saturday night and I can't."

"Do you have a son or daughter?" Dessie asked.

"Daughter, and every bit of a woman as I have ever seen!"

"Well, she'll have big fun playing with Iren, my son. He's seven months old, and already he is a charmer!" Stephen wrote down his name and address for Dessie. She promised to be at his place on Friday. She could hardly wait to tell Sharon about this amazing guy she had met, and was now invited to his study group.

"Well it's about time! I thought you were just sitting, waiting to dry up like a raisin!"

"Shut up girl! I never had any intention of letting any part of me dry up like a raisin! If you could see this guy, you would think that he was God's gift to women everywhere!"

"While we're on that subject, is he seeing someone right now?" Dessie looked puzzled for a moment.

"I don't think so," she said, "at least he didn't give any indication that he was. I'm almost certain that he isn't because he mentioned having to keep his two year old daughter on the weekends. I sure would like to find out more about him!"

"Slow down girl! You're moving too fast! Let him discover you. If you just keep doing what you're doing, he'll come around. Now aren't you glad that I made your lazy behind go to the gym with me?" Dessie laughed and threw a pillow from the couch; hitting Sharon as they recalled the first time that they went.

DC

By that Friday, Dessie was as giddy as a schoolgirl on her first date. She managed to get home, play with Iren and take a soothing, hot bath.

She put on a plain, navy blue business dress with a gold brooch at the neck. She completed her look with a wool sweater/jacket in faded blue with navy blue trim.

Just as she finished dressing, Sharon was walking in with Ben. "Have fun at your study group," Sharon said, with a knowing wink. Dessie wanted to get her for that, but she couldn't say anything because Ben was there.

"I'll see you guys in an hour or so," Dessie said as she headed out of the door.

With his apartment not being that far, she was able to get there in little less than fifteen minutes.

Once there, Dessie searched for Stephen's name, found it, rang his bell, and was immediately let in. Dessie walked upstairs to apartment 205. A door opened and a woman walked out of it looking angry and telling someone behind her that it wasn't *'traditional.'*

Stephen invited Dessie into the apartment; telling her that some of the others were already inside. A few moments passed before he came back to the living room.

"Sorry about that guys," Stephen stated to the group, 'baby mama drama!' a couple of the guys acknowledged, and were supportive of his plight.

The group didn't waste any time in getting down to the reason why they were there. They dissected their notes from the two previous classes so that everyone was on one accord. Anything that was not understood was saved for the very end so that it could be discussed without taking up precious time reserved for learning the dynamics of the course. Dessie was trying hard to think of something that she could ask about at the end of the session so that she could spend a minute or two talking to Stephen.

By the end of the study session, Dessie still hadn't thought of anything involved in the course so far that they hadn't already touched on. She decided that she was going to ask him what area of law he was interested in, and what area he felt was best suited for women.

As soon as most of the group bid them goodnight, Dessie posed her question.

"What did you earn your Bachelor's in?" he asked.

"Business Administration."

"Corporate, Real Estate, but you don't have to limit yourself to those areas. I have a Business degree also, but my true calling is a Civil Attorney. I didn't realize what my calling was until I almost lost all rights to my daughter. An ugly divorce was just the beginning! When I witnessed what was happening to me, I didn't want to see another person go through what I went through. All I wanted was to be able to see my daughter; to have her in my life."

"So your lawyer saw to it that you have those rights?"

"She sure did, and I thank God for her every single day. I still have my rights as a parent!" Dessie was enthralled by his passion as he spoke of his daughter.

"Where is your little girl? Did she come this weekend?" Dessie asked.

"Yes, she's here. Would you like to meet her?" Dessie nodded yes as she followed him to a door. He tapped on it and walked in. a little girl with a pink dress and white tights; with pink and white barrettes in her hair, ran to Stephen and was up in his arms in a flash. "Dessie this is my daughter Daisha. Daisha say "hi" to Dessie.

"Well it's about time!" a masculine voice said, causing Dessie to search the room to see where the voice was coming from. A young slender guy appeared almost as instantly as his voice had. He walked directly to Stephen and Daisha and embraced them both, kissing Stephen fully on the lips. It seemed to Dessie as if she had been standing there for a long, long time.

"Dessie, these are the loves of my life!" Stephen said, "This is Trevin and my pretty baby daughter!" It all came back to her; the scene at the door, the harsh comments concerning 'traditional.' It all became clear at that moment.

Dessie couldn't believe what she had just witnessed. There was absolutely no way she would have believed that Stephen was gay. It just couldn't be! The way he looked at her, the way he talked to her. It just couldn't be!

Dessie didn't recall leaving Stephen's apartment, but she did feel the chilly air on her face; causing her eyes to tear up. She didn't bother to wipe them. She continued walking home. Once there, she walked in and she saw Ben on the floor with Iren. She told them that she needed lie down for a few minutes and rushed into her room and got on the bed without taking off her coat. A short while later, Sharon knocked on the bedroom door and walked in holding Iren. "I sent Ben home Dess. Is something wrong?" When Dessie was able to form the words, she told Sharon what had occurred, and how she felt about it.

"What are you upset about? I think the brother was painfully honest. A lot of brothers would have led you into thinking that they were all about you; when in fact they wanted to be you! Count your blessing! It didn't happen this time, but maybe next time..."

"I just can't understand how I didn't see it." Dessie flatly stated.

"Dessie, listen to me, you didn't see it because you weren't looking for it. You might not have seen anything had it not been for their open display of affection. A lot of guys can't even begin to tell anybody that they like to groove with other men. There's a guy who works out of my office, and we all know that he's gay. He doesn't even attempt to hide who he is. He doesn't look feminine; he doesn't wear perfume or talk the way we think they should. He is the only worker that we have who is willing to deal with AIDS cases, and do you know what he has to say about all this pain and suffering?"

"What?"

"Most of them were too afraid to come out and be themselves. They end up looking for sex and affection in the seamiest places; from folks that they would probably never lay eyes on again. Most of them don't know from whom they were infected. Count your blessings. They are in your favor!" Dessie felt so much better after their talk. How could she be anything but up? Stephen was happy, and if he could be happy with all he had to face, she knew that she had reasons to rejoice.

Dessie managed to keep up with her studies, her job and Iren. He was getting so big; she could hardly handle him by herself. More of his hair had grown in to the point that Dessie could now braid it.

Dessie was nursing him one evening when he suddenly bit her nipple; making her scream in agony. She wanted to spank him, but he wouldn't even know what he was getting spanked for. He was laughing the whole time while Dessie inspected the damage he'd done. "That's it buddy! From now on, you'll get your milk from a bottle from me too!" Iren seemed to be overjoyed when his mother talked to him, kicking his legs and moving his arms wildly.

Every day he seemed to look more and more like Ray. It saddened her to think that one day she would have to tell him that his father never wanted him. She didn't want to lie to him. When he was old enough to understand, she would tell him the truth. No matter how hard it would hurt.

DC

During the latter part of February, Dessie was given notice that a very important deposition was to take place, and that she needed to get several files together since this was a criminal matter as well as a possible, huge, civil suit. It was going to be extensive. She was instructed to make sure that the water cooler in the conference room was full; plenty of coffee and legal pads and pens. The case involved the brutal beating of a young Black man by several white police officers in a public park in broad daylight. Dessie had recalled hearing it on the news.

They had thought that he was a vagrant when in fact he was on a lunch break from the high school where he taught. The papers were loaded with accounts of what happened from the sensational to the pristine descriptions recorded in the *New York Times*. What shocked Dessie the most, were the photographs that were taken of the young teacher. The daily news could describe how brutally he was beaten, but nothing could compare to the photographs that Dessie had held in her own hands. Just looking at them made her wince and brought tears to her own eyes.

On the morning of the deposition, one of the senior attorneys informed Dessie that two of the officers had been involved in a similar incident about three years earlier. They had handled the case against them then. He asked her to go to the files and see what she could dig up. Dessie started to page the secretary to pass the task off to her, but the partner turned around and told her that he wanted only her on the assignment. He further told her that she was to bring the files directly to him as soon as she located them. "But what should I do if you are already in the deposition?" Dessie asked.

"Bring them right in as soon as you locate them!" he rushed back to his office and shut the door.

It took Dessie at least forty-five minutes to pull all the files together. She walked into the conference room crowded with lawyers, the victim, and a stenographer. She took a cursory glance around the room to locate the attorney that requested the files. She took them over to him as soon as she spotted him. She turned to leave the room, and almost stopped in her tracks. Sitting across the table, intently staring at her, sat Darryl! She left the room as quickly as she could.

Back at her desk, she didn't know what to do. It seemed as if every nerve she had was on edge. Dessie informed the secretary that she taking an early lunch, and that she had several errands to run for the office and she didn't know when she would be back.

She didn't know why she was running from him. Any emotional ties that they might have had were severed a long time ago. He had moved on in his life, and she had done the same. She had no explanation for feeling the way she did. She just did.

Two hours later, she returned to the office hoping that the deposition had been completed. She felt that there was just a small chance of that since most of them can last for hours, and even days for that matter. She took the elevator up to the office; silently praying that Darryl was gone. When she sat at her desk, she saw that there were several messages for her. She carefully breathed as she searched through the messages, looking for the one that bore Darryl's name on it. Relieved, actually, almost disappointed, none of them were from him. The conference room was empty. She was now able to relax from all the stress.

When Dessie left work two hours later, she still hadn't heard anything from Darryl. She headed into the chill evening air for home. Suddenly, someone firmly grabbed her arm. She turned slightly and looked up into Darryl's strong, handsome face. "Hello Mrs. Cunningham!" Darryl said.

"What are you doing here Darryl?"

"I was waiting on you to come out. Plus, I work here."

"In this building?" Dessie questioned.

"Not too far from here."

"That's a relief! I don't have to worry about running into you every day!"

"Why the attitude? We're old friends aren't we?" Dessie snickered and shook her head.

"After the way you treated me? You want to call yourself a *friend*?"

"Why don't we go somewhere for coffee and get out of the cold?"

"I don't drink coffee!" Dessie said hotly.

"They serve tea also," Darryl said, with a pleading look in his eyes. "If I could just talk to you for ten or fifteen minutes. Please?" Dessie reached into her purse to retrieve her cell phone to call Etta to let her know that she was going to be late. She didn't call out any names, so Darryl didn't know whom she was talking to.

"There's a nice deli not too far from here. We can sit in there and talk." Dessie and he walked down the street without acknowledging each other's presence. When they reached the deli, Darryl opened the door and motioned for Dessie to go inside. They chose a booth in the back of the establishment. Darryl asked her what type of tea she would like.

"Anything herbal." Was her reply. When Darryl returned to the table, Dessie had taken off her coat and gloves to reveal a navy blue turtleneck sweater dress. She didn't want to wear it to work, but the heating system had been acting up since the day before, and she didn't want to freeze another day.

Darryl sat looking at her, almost afraid to speak. When he did, he surprised himself. "I've thought about you almost every single day since I left Virginia," Darryl told her, "I was such a fool for losing you the way that I did."

"You weren't the fool. I was. I was foolish to think that you really wanted to be with me."

"Why are you saying that Dess? I know what I did was wrong, but I *did* love you!" Darryl said firmly.

"If you loved me, that girl would not have been in your room. It only reinforced what I believed all along."

"And, what is that, may I ask?"

"The only thing that you wanted was a piece of ass! I was a freshman; away from home for the very first time, and you're pressuring me to have sex. Did it ever dawn on you that I was already coping with enough changes without having to deal with a boyfriend who seemed only interested in sex?"

"So you remember coming to my room and seeing Kim there?" infuriated, Dessie stood up to leave.

"I know you didn't have me come here to gloat over your sexual accomplishments!" Dessie stated.

"Not at all Dessie! I don't need anyone's validation on that! Now, would you please sit down and hear me out?" Dessie reluctantly sat back down.

"You came over to my room because you wanted me too!" Dessie started to say something, but Darryl stopped her. "Let me finish please! I was being selfish; thinking only of myself before I thought about you.

You were the first girl that I had ever been serious about. I thought that you wanted me in the same way."

"Maybe I did Darryl, but being pressured into it, is just about equal to being raped. That picture destroyed what I thought we had."

"I'm so sorry for that Dess. I didn't mean to destroy us. I was only trying to enhance the love that we had for each other."

"That's what I'm trying to understand Darryl. If you had truly loved me, why couldn't getting intimate wait?" she asked.

"All I can say about that Dess is that I was young and immature. Older guys were telling me to 'hit it,' do this, do that. I wanted you, but not for the reasons that they were suggesting. I had already had sex before I met you. I didn't want to have sex just to be *'having it'* anymore. I loved you, and I wanted you to want me just as much."

Dessie studied his handsome face for a few moments and she decided that what he was saying was the truth.

"I see that you have moved on with your life; married now; any children?"

"I was sorry to learn of your wife's passing. She was pretty young," Dessie said, steering the conversation away from her.

"Twenty-four years old to be exact. She was a beautiful person. Always trying to give of herself; even as she lay dying."

Darryl's face told of the agony that she and he must have gone through.

"She didn't want me to be sad and lonely. She would call some of my friends up and beg them to come and take me out to the gym or dinner, or anything that was going to take me away from her pain and suffering."

"How long had you two been together?" Dessie asked.

"We met two years ago, and were married a year later. Just before our wedding, we found out about the cancer. Janice wanted to call off the wedding, but I refused. I loved her, and I wasn't going to leave her. There was always hope that the cancer wouldn't take her life."

"I'm touched by her bravery. She must have loved you so much." Dessie told him.

"We loved each other with all we had to give. The only thing that we couldn't do was have a child, but Janice even had that figured out. Once she got well, we were going to adopt some children. What about you Dess? I've been sitting here talking about me all along. What about you? You're married now. That much I do know, but do you and your husband have any children?"

"I...we have an eight month old son."

"Does he look like you?" he asked.

"Not at all! He is every bit his father's son," Dessie said as she looked at her watch. "Wow! Its seven o'clock! I didn't realize that we had sat here all this time!" Dessie said as she stood up, and Darryl took her coat to assist her in putting it on. She had forgotten how tall he was. She had on heels and he was still a head taller than she was. He walked her to the subway. He told her that he had an eight o'clock dinner engagement and wouldn't be going home for quite some time.

"Would it be okay if I called you sometime? I feel like I've lost an old friend and found her again. I'm not trying to push up on you or anything. I just want us to be friends. I made a terrible mistake back in Virginia, and I apologize for that. Can you forgive me?" Dessie looked up at him for a few seconds before she spoke. Her emotions were playing havoc with her mind and her heart.

"I forgive you Darryl." They both seemed to reach out and embrace each other at the same time; both with their own personal pain. Dessie headed down the stairs without answering his request. He watched her leave. She never looked back.

DC

"...From what he told me, she was a very unselfish person."

"I will agree on that," Sharon said, "every time I talked with her, she was more concerned about how I was doing than how she was feeling."

"I feel so sorry for him," Dessie said, with a heavy sigh, "but only he knows what it is really like to lose someone in the manner that he did."

"How did he look?" Sharon asked.

"Seriously attractive. When I first walked into the conference room, I wasn't paying attention as to who all was there, but when I was leaving, he was staring so hard; I could feel his eyes on me. He had on oversize frames, and he had this kind of shocked look on his face. Girl! I have to admit it; the brother is sexy as hell!"

"So tell me, why do you *not* want to see him again?"

"I don't... I don't know how to answer that. What we had was so long ago, I doubt that we could really be friends. The timing is all wrong and..."

"You told him that that you were married," Sharon finished for her.

"That too, but I also know that he's lonely, and I don't want to be a part of someone's life to replace what they lost."

"I can understand that," Sharon said, "but you can't be sure unless he actually comes out and says that."

"He probably has plenty of women chasing after him; he's successful and he looks it."

"I still think that you should have told him the truth."

"I'll keep him in mind should I have this overwhelming desire to reconnect to the past!" Sharon threw Iten's plush ball that found its mark in Dessie's Back.

"I'm going to call and tell him everything! Including you are still in love with him! Sharon shouted as Dessie threw the ball back at her.

"Girrrl! And when you do, like we use to say down home," Dessie said with an accentuated drawl, "your soul belongs to Jesus, but yo ass belongs to me!" they talked and laughed until Iren woke up. He rarely woke up in the night; sleeping right through to five or six in the morning. Dessie didn't think that this time would ever come.

Chapter Seven

"So when are you leaving?" Debra asked Vicki, as they worked out on the stationary bikes.

"The nineteenth of next month. I can hardly believe that I'm actually going. I've dreamed of this trip ever since I was little. We use to go to this five and dime store and they would have this dark blue bottle of perfume, or toilet water called *"Evening in Paris,"* Debra started laughing and nodding her head up and down remembering that same dark blue bottle, "I believe everybody's mother in the neighborhood had one of those bottles!"

"Or four or five depending on how many children she had!" Debra finished.

"I was mesmerized by that bottle. I can't ever remember what it smelled like, but the mysterious etching on the bottle enchanted me. Now, I'm finally going to have an *"Evening in Paris."*

"You go Girl! My dream trip is to visit Africa someday. It's really an adventuresome trip, but the cost is way too much for me to try and pay for now. I think I'll give myself a year, maybe a year and a half to finance it."

"You should post a sign in the church inviting anyone whose interested to a meeting to discuss the possibility of going as a group," Vicki suggested, "it would be a lot cheaper than doing it by yourself."

"Sounds like a plan to me. When I get home, I'll run a couple of announcements off to plan a meeting for anyone who might be interested."

"Maybe you should first visit a couple of travel agencies and see what they have to offer. That way, you'll have some information to draw them into the idea."

"You know what Vicki?"

"What?"

"I really do like your ideas! I'm going to take it a step further and make up a poster board display with pictures and brochures, and then we can go and have a meeting about when, where, and how."

"Shoot, hearing you talking about it; I may just go along for the ride myself!" Vicki informed her friend.

After their time on the bikes, they opted for the mineral bath hot tub. When they got in the tub, the only one's that were in it were an elderly couple who didn't pay Vicki and Debra any attention.

"Did Sharon tell you that Dessie saw Darryl and they sat and talked for hours?" Debra asked Vicki.

"She told me that they ran into each other, but she didn't tell me that they actually talked at length."

"Sharon told me that Dessie didn't really take the whole thing seriously. Dessie feels that Darryl is only looking for some female companionship, and she doesn't want to be seen as a substitute. Plus, Sharon said that she told him that she was happily married with a young baby."

"What! Is she crazy or something? Do she know that the brother is a successful lawyer with a Brooklyn Heights address?"

"I don't think that matters to her." Debra informed Vicki.

"When news leaks out that he's available and successful..."

"Don't forget straight Girl!" Debra threw in.

"And straight, he'll have to beat the she-devils off him! Shit! I might even submit an application myself!" Vicki jokingly threw in.

"Yeah, I bet you will! You're always looking for a big, huge, ample... wallet!"

"And what's wrong with that? I prefer to fall in love with men who can take care of me!"

"Well, what in the world are you doing with Jeff? He *ain't* got no money!"

"Believe me, with him, I don't care if he don't have two nickels to rub together! The brother *can* take care of me!" Vicki and Debra were laughing so hard that the elderly couple sat staring at them.

"Lets get out of here," Vicki suggested, "I have an appointment at Metamorphosis over on East 60th St. for a massage and a facial. Wanna come?"

"Naw. That's okay. I have to get my mother and take her shopping. I can drop you off if you want me to." Debra said, as they left the bath.

"That'll work, but you really need to come and try their cinnamon facial scrub. It makes your skin glow."

"Maybe next time. We can book an appointment together," Debra told Vicki as she pulled up to the day spa to let her out, "later Girl!"

"Later!" Vicki hollered back, as Debra pulled off.

DC

Two weeks after their chance meeting, Darryl called Dessie's office to invite her and her husband out to dinner. Dessie was taken aback by the unexpected phone call. Before she knew it, he had a commitment from her to join him and a guest for dinner. "There's someone that I want you to meet." Darryl told her.

"Who?" Dessie asked.

"If I told you, maybe you wouldn't be interested in coming." Dessie was curious, and wanted to know exactly who it was.

"Are you trying to introduce me to someone you intend to marry? Cause if you are, I can tell you right now that I'm not the least bit interested in your personal life!"

"I swear to you Dessie, that is not the case. I merely want us to be friends. There's no harm in that, is there? Besides I'm inviting both your husband and yourself for a fine evening of dining and conversation. It couldn't be more platonic than that," he explained.

"I just find this whole dinner invitation thing to be out of character for two people who have not spoken to each other in years."

"Dessie, lets try to forget the past and be friends. I sincerely mean that." He didn't wait for her to respond before stating his plans. "I've booked us a table for four at 'Miss Mamie's Spoonbread Too' at West 110th Street for Thursday at seven. Take care and I'll see you then!"

Dessie sat holding a dead phone; wondering what excuse she was going to use to get out of meeting Darryl and whoever for dinner. The bigger question looming in her head, was whom could she get to play her husband on such a short notice?

"Hell no! I told you before we left to come up here that I wasn't going to take part in any more of your wild ass schemes!" Sharon strongly stated to her worried roommate.

"Sharon you have got to help me! Just this once and I'll promise to never involve you in anything else!" Sharon wasn't moved by her friend's desperate pleas.

"Now you can see what I mean about one lie leading to another, and it'll only keep growing. Why would you agree to go to dinner with him anyway?" Sharon asked.

"When he said that there was someone he wanted me to meet, and he wouldn't tell me his or her name; I guess being nosey pulled me right in."

"I can't let you involve Ben. Number one, I don't believe he'll do it, and number two, he's working on a major project and won't be available for quite some time."

"What about Diane's husband? Maybe he could do it for me."

"Now I know that you have lost your mind for real! Diane would kill you and me too! Don't mess around with her husband if you want to live!"

"What am I going to do?" Dessie almost screamed, "I can't let him find out that I lied about being married!"

"I don't know what you're going to do about all this, but I know one thing, and that is you're not to involve Ben and I into any of your stuff!"

"I heard you the first time Sharon!" Dessie said, almost angrily. Sharon didn't care if she was angry. She was not going to be implicated in any more of Dessie's failed attempts at trying to make things right.

"I'll have something figured out by Thursday evening."

"I have no doubt that you will!" Sharon said.

or the next couple of days, Dessie tried to think of someone she could ask to play the role of a substitute husband/father. She had wanted to ask Stephen but she felt that Darryl would have been able to see right through him. She came up with a simple plan that was going to have to do.

𝒟𝒞

Dessie found the restaurant without any trouble. Darryl and his guest, a young light-skinned woman were already seated when she was shown to the reserved table. Darryl was out of his seat immediately, and looking past Dessie as he helped her remove her coat. "Where is your husband? I thought he was joining us tonight."

"Oh he'll be here. He had to work late this evening, but he should meet us here by seven thirty." Dessie explained.

"This is Samantha Darden, Dessie, my guest this evening."

"Darryl you are so silly!" the young woman said, "he knows that I'm much more to him than that! Mother said that in six month's time, he will be my husband!" the woman moved her chair even closer to Darryl's; as if that was at all possible. Dessie cut her eyes at Darryl after the woman said they were to be married. Darryl shook his head slightly and stiffly as if letting Dessie know that what she was saying wasn't true. "When we get married, daddy says that Darryl would probably

115

make partner." The woman said, smiling at Darryl. "What does your husband do for a living Dorrie?" Samantha asked.

"My name is "Dessie.""

"Oh! I'm so sorry! Mother said that if she didn't tell me what day it was at least twice, I wouldn't even know that!" Samantha said, laughing at her own corny attempt to sound witty. "So Dessie, what does your husband do?" Samantha asked again.

"He's a Financial Planner."

"Oh! He works at a bank! Which one?"

Dessie looked at Darryl.

"He doesn't work at a bank. He works at an insurance company." Dessie told her, with a hint of indignation in her voice.

"Well that's stupid! What would a financial planner be doing at an insurance company?" Dessie looked at her without saying a word. Feeling awkward by the silence, Dessie asked Samantha what school she attended.

"Vassar!" Samantha said proudly.

"What was your major there?" Dessie continued.

"I was a Liberal Artist, but I haven't been able to get one single job working in a museum yet! Daddy told me not to worry about it; we have more than enough money!"

"To do what?" Dessie asked. Samantha just looked at her blankly. Just as Dessie was about to ask her again, a waitress came to their table with four menus.

"I'm so sorry," the waitress said, "I was told that this table was for a party of four."

"That's okay ma'am," Dessie spoke up, "my husband is a little late, but he should be here any minute now." The waitress gave them each a menu and placed the fourth at the empty place setting. Dessie silently prayed that Debra would do what she had promised. Looking over the menu, Dessie commented about the many soul food entrees the restaurant offered.

"Oh! Oh! Let me tell you something Dorrie!" Samantha excitedly said, "one day I called Darryl at the office and invited him to dinner since mother and father had a dinner engagement that evening. I asked Darryl what he wanted to eat for dinner and he said that he felt like having some soul food. I said okay, and sent the maid to my favorite Korean restaurant. I ordered this fabulous ten-course meal. When Darryl arrived at the house, I had everything set up and I had the maid bring on the goodies. Well, Darryl just sat there looking at all this food. He asked what it was, and I told him that it was the Seoul food that he wanted. I don't think he knew what to say! I was eating like I had never tasted this stuff before. He finally told me what kind of 'soul food' he meant. I was so embarrassed; I didn't know what to do! I told Mother the next day what had happened, and she told me not to worry about it because if he kept eating all of his kind of soul food, he would eventually turn into a soul himself! Whatever that means!"

-While Samantha laughed, Dessie stared in disbelief at Darryl. He couldn't be serious about this person. She could hardly wait to find out from him what this nonsense was all about, and why was he trying to pull her into it.

At seven thirty sharp, Dessie's cell phone started to ring quite audibly. She reached into her purse to retrieve it. "Oh hello Honey! What's keeping you so long?" Dessie asked. "How much longer do you think you'll be?" an exasperated look appeared on Dessie's face. "I know," Dessie paused for a moment, "sure Honey, I'll let them know. I'll see you sometime tonight when you get home." Dessie looked at Darryl as she flipped her phone closed. "Paul won't be able to join us this evening. He has to work overtime."

"I guess you guys must need the money because Daddy says the only people who worked overtime, were those hopelessly in debt or those who were not able to live on the money they made in their regular nine to five!" Dessie gave her a look that conveyed the message that she was ready to beat her brains out, or whatever she had in her head. *Brains would have been an upgrade in her case!*

"I'm sorry about that Dess. I was looking forward to meeting Mr. Cunningham this evening." Darryl said, but the way that he said the name 'Cunningham;' gave one a reason to doubt that there was such a person. Dessie acted as if she had not heard the inflection in his voice, "maybe he can join us on another occasion," Darryl graciously offered, "but do take him some dinner home. I'm sure that he will appreciate the gesture."

"Thank you Darryl! I'll do that!" When it came time for them to order, Dessie ordered an extra meal to go of smothered pork chops, rice, string beans and coconut cake. She tried to act like it was an everyday thing, but Darryl kept at her as if he didn't believe her. She assumed. What she didn't believe was how he could possibly even begin to consider this half-wit for marriage. *This has got to be some sort of joke! Somebody is going to jump up soon and say 'April fool!'* Dessie thought.

When she couldn't take anymore of the insane chatter from Samantha, she informed them that she was tired and that she had to get home to her husband and son. She thanked Darryl for a wonderful evening with ice in her voice. He promised that he would call her soon. As soon as her back was turned, Dessie heard Samantha say that she was "so stuck up!" and she was glad that Dessie had left. Dessie started to turn around and really give her something to talk about, but decided that the idiot wasn't worth a scene.

𝒟𝒞

"I don't know what he was thinking Sharon. It's really beyond me as to why he was even out with this overgrown, spoiled child. You wouldn't believe how hopelessly sheltered this girl has been. I tried not to show how angered I was to be in their company, but I'm positive that Darryl knows my feelings, and won't ever invite me out again. What I can't understand is why he would still invite me out when I told him that if he was inviting me out to meet someone that he intended on marrying, I wasn't interested."

"Why would you just come out of the blue and ask him a question like that?" asked Sharon.

"I just felt that he might be up to something like that. You know... like trying to make me jealous or something."

"I don't see how or why he would do that. You did tell him that you were married right?"

"Yeah. I did tell him that."

"So, I don't see how he could have set this situation up to agitate you. You said that she was the one talking marriage and not him."

"Right, but he didn't say anything to contradict her marriage statement."

"I just think you're overreacting to the whole thing. He works for her dad's law firm, and maybe she thinks that whatever belongs to daddy belongs to her as well. We do have folks in this world who think just like that. They have never been denied anything and that attitude prevails in all aspects of their lives."

"I just can't see how Darryl, with all the brain power that he possesses, would give Samantha a fraction of his time."

"Stranger things have happened." Sharon concluded, as she went off to bed. Dessie went into her room and stood at her son's crib for the longest time. It amazed her to see how much he had grown. He was such a happy baby. She gently kissed him good night.

Chapter Eight

Dessie informed the receptionist that any calls that came in for her that were not of a business nature; she was to take a message, "unless it's my sitter, Mrs. Johnson, then put the call through." Dessie was determined to not let any distractions outside of work related issues, interfere with her job performance. She had made up her mind to re-double her efforts at attaining a degree in law. It meant taking two courses the following semester, but no matter how hard it was going to be in getting them done, she needed to do it. She couldn't see herself being a high paid 'go for' for the rest of her life.

By the time she returned from lunch, Darryl had called five times, and Etta had called once. Thinking that something was wrong with the baby, Dessie rushed to dial the numbers that would bring her closer to her son. "There's nothing wrong here," Etta told her, "your mother called and said that it's important that she speak to you. She said that it is not an emergency though." Dessie's heart started to slow once she realized that everything was fine with Iren. She reached into her purse just as she was saying bye to Etta to get her cell phone and call Ruthie.

"Hey Baby! How you doing?" Ruthie asked.

"I'm okay Mama. How about you?"

"Everything with me is fine. I have twelve gowns that I'm working on for the ball in May, but I'm okay with them. Most of them only need detail work, and that ain't hard to do."

"How's everybody doing there Mama? Is Aunt Beatrice home yet?"

"Just about everybody is fine except for Patrice. She pregnant now. She won't tell nobody who the baby daddy is, but Brent says that Wesley is the child's daddy." Dessie was dumbfounded at the revelation.

"Is she still living there with you Mama?"

"Naw child! She ain't lived here since I don't know when! Brent says she there at the house with Wesley, and Bea is in the nursing home getting well." Dessie was surprised that her mother was able to speak so calmly about Patrice and Wesley. It was almost as if she wasn't shocked at all about the fact that her niece and sister's boyfriend were involved in a scandalous affair. "The doctor told Bea that if she ever took another drink, she would be killing herself. Bea sat there and didn't say a word. I don't know if she was listening or not. The feeling that I got from Bea was that she didn't care one way or the other. What little bit of money that she had, the county took that from the bank to help pay her hospital bill, and it didn't cover that much. She's on the county now."

"Mama, you mean to tell me that out of a hundred thousand dollars, that Aunt Beatrice don't have any of it left?"

"Nope. Not a dime, and all of 'em that helped her spend it, not one of them came to sit by her bed while she laid there suffering." Dessie's eyes were filled with tears after her mother had told her of the events that had taken place in her aunt's life.

"Does she know about Patrice and Wesley Mama?"

"Not as far as I know Dessie, but it's just a matter of time before Bea finds out, and start drinking again and go on and die. I keep on paying her burial policy so that I have something to bury her with. I don't have to cry no more. I did all of that already. I looked at Bea the other day, and there was nothing left in her. Everything is already gone. Ain't nothing left but a empty shell."

"I'm so sorry to hear all of this Mama, but I know that you have done all that you could, and the rest is left up to Aunt Beatrice and God."

It was rare when Ruthie gave up on something, but Dessie could feel it in her mother's voice, and that made her know that it was almost futile to wish for things to be different. At that very moment, Dessie wanted to tell her about Iren, but she felt that it would send Ruthie over the edge instead of bringing joy from this new life that she had also made possible.

When Dessie hung up the phone, she went into the ladies room and cried for a few minutes for the plight that her family was now facing. Afterwards, Dessie finished up with the work on her desk, and made sure that everything she needed for Monday was right at hand.

She ran into the cleaning woman, Nilda, on her way out and stopped to tell her to make sure she cleaned all the toilet bowls in both the ladies and men's rooms. If Dessie didn't tell her, she wouldn't do them. Dessie made a mental note to put the directive in writing, and have one of the other office workers witness it so that if Nilda comes up with the "Nobody ever told me" line, or "Me no understand you English."

Nilda had tried to pull that one on her the month before when she had told her to do something and she didn't want to do it. Dessie walked in on her in the conference room with her feet up on the table while she was speaking perfect English to someone on the phone. Dessie wrote down the time and date and when the phone bill came, she compared the information that she had with the phone bill and found that the cleaning woman had been calling Puerto Rico almost every evening; sitting around talking sometimes as long as an hour or more. Dessie went to her with the detailed bill and demanded that she pay it or she would bring it to the attention of her superiors. When Nilda saw that she was not fooling, she immediately started giving Dessie a portion of her paycheck each week to make up the deficit. Dessie hated to do things this way, but since she had direct control of the operating account, she was not to going to let Nilda's impropriety put her own position in jeopardy. To safeguard against any future incidents of this nature, Dessie contacted the phone company and got a new phone plan put into place. Before any long distance calls could be made, a three-digit code had to be entered after the number or the call was immediately disconnected.

Dessie took the middle elevator down to the main floor of the office building. Surprisingly, there was no one else on it. *Why should there be? Dessie thought, everybody seemed to have a life that they shared with others. She only had Iren when it came down to it, and every single thing that she did, was somehow, going to always affect her beautiful son.*

When the doors of the elevator opened, Darryl was standing right in front of it looking somewhat angry. "Do you have any idea how many times I've called you today?" he said, with a hint of anger in his voice. Dessie just looked up into his face without answering him. She stepped out of the elevator to walk past him; when he blocked her movement.

"I want you to tell me why you would not return my calls today?" Darryl asked firmly.

"Darryl," Dessie began, "why would I owe you an explanation on anything that I do, or don't do? I'm married and I'm by no means responsible to you! I instructed the receptionist to inform any callers that I was tied up with other matters, and only emergency calls were to be put through," Dessie said, as she tried to walk around him.

"I considered my call to be an emergency in nature," he said, as she moved towards the door, "I think being in love with you warrants a call back!" Dessie stopped dead in her tracks, "I've never stopped loving you. You've never given me the chance to correct the mistakes of the past." Dessie slowly turned to face the man that meant everything to her at a time that seemed so long ago.

"How can you say that Darryl? I'm no longer available to you." Darryl walked to her to close the gap between them, and to keep those nearby from hearing their conversation.

"I know the truth Dessie. I know that you are not married." Angrily, she questioned him on how he would know that. "Remember when we went to sign up for our room assignments before we broke up?" Dessie listened without interrupting him. "When we filled out the forms, I remembered your mother's maiden name was Cunningham, and I figured it was too much of a coincidence for you to marry someone with that last name. I looked for a marriage license in your state and couldn't come up with one. I wanted to be absolutely positive before I approached you." Dessie stood staring into his face with tear filled eyes. "I still love you Dessie. I never stopped. I want to have another chance with you so that I can be the man you want me to be." Darryl embraced her, and she didn't resist. She felt that she was at a familiar place. It felt like she had been missing a part of herself, and she had finally found it after searching for so long.

DC

"Of course you're going to like him Mama!

He's sweet, kind and loving, and he truly loves me!" an excited Dessie told her mother.

"When am I going to get a chance to meet this man that you are so in love with?"

"We'll be there in a few weeks so that you can fit me for my gown, and remember Mama, I don't want anything too extravagant," Dessie implored.

"Child, it's only once in a lifetime that your only daughter gets married and you can make her gown yourself!"

"I know Mama, I know, but we don't want anything to take away from the solemnity of the moment. Most of the gowns that I've looked at in the bridal magazines so far are strapless and sleek. Not the traditional wedding look."

"When you get here, we'll look over some patterns and magazines and you can choose whichever one you like."

"I talked to Tasha last week Mama, and she said that she didn't care what she had to do to get that weekend off, but she was going to be home so that she could be my maid of honor. I'm so happy Mama! I haven't seen Tasha in so long I don't know if I'll even recognize her!"

"Child you'll know Tasha if it was pitch black out and raining tar! Ya'll will know each other, but what about those invitations you wanted to send?" Ruthie asked.

"Oh yeah! I just need for you to get me addresses of those that you want to invite from the church."

"Most people that be getting married round here just stand up after the church service and invite the whole church to the wedding."

"I don't want you doing that Mama. I want to send each person an invitation."

"That's gonna cost you a pretty penny Dessie Lee!" Ruthie intoned.

"That's not a problem Mama. My husband to be is very well off, and money is one thing we don't have to worry about."

"Just cause you don't have to worry about it don't mean you should just up and waste it either Child!" Dessie laughed at Ruthie's chastisement.

"Mama it is okay! The invitations are the cheapest things we have to get for the wedding!"

"I'll never understand how young folks can waste so much money on nothing!" Ruthie said, and Dessie laughed at. She had never felt such exhilaration as she felt at that moment.

The night that Darryl proposed to her was so unexpected and so different from what she expected a proposal to be. She was studying for an exam and Darryl had Iren on the floor playing and laughing. They took to each other the second that they had met. Darryl often sat holding Iren until he fell asleep; sometimes lingering over him when he should have long been gone.

Iren approached Dessie, tapping her on her leg and saying 'Mom,' or what sounded like mom. Either way, he made sure that you knew he was there. Dessie at first wasn't paying much attention to him, but he wouldn't leave her alone. She looked down to see what he wanted, and he held up the most fantastic diamond that she had ever seen. She took the ring from Iren and looked at Darryl. He sat staring at her with a look of uncertainty and anticipation on his face. Finally, he said "Well..." and she ran into his arms crying and saying 'yes' over and over.

DC

"And just how do you plan on doing that?" Sharon asked Dessie.

"Etta has already promised me that she will keep Iren for the two weeks that we are going to be away," Dessie explained.

"Dessie you know that that is not what I'm talking about. How long are you going to be able to keep Iren hidden from your family?" Dessie started pacing around the room in an agitated manner.

"I know that I'm not going to be able to hide him forever, and I don't plan to. I just have to find the way to tell my mother. I have hurt her so many times that I know one more might just break her down for good."

"I understand what you are saying, but you are not hearing me." Sharon said.

"What do you want me to do about it right now Sharon?" a frustrated Dessie asked. "I'm doing all that I can to get this wedding together, keeping my job, taking care of Iren, and trying to spend time with Darryl when I can."

"All that I'm saying Dessie, is for you to take care of your responsibilities without your mother finding out about your situation from an unconcerned source who wouldn't care who they hurt. You better get a plan B together just in case."

"Darryl and I are working on that right now Sharon. He has offered to have Iren's name changed after we are married, but I don't know if I want to do that. I gave my son my grandparents name so that the name lives on. I'm not really keen on taking it away from him.

"You can always hyphen the name with Darryl's surname." Sharon suggested.

"That's a good idea," Dessie said, "but I don't know about doing that because I don't want Ray to ever be able to find him. I don't plan on seeing Ray once I get back home. I don't want his money, and the only reason that I might contact him about it is that I believe a man should be responsible for what he helped create."

"If I were you Dessie, I would drop the matter entirely. It's obvious that you no longer need his money, and seeking him out for it is only going to cause more pain, and open up old wounds."

"I guess the only way that I'm going to heal is to let go of all the hostility that I feel for him. Besides, my life has a greater meaning now that Darryl has come back into my life. I love him with every thing that's in me. Things have improved so much until sometimes, I don't know if I am awake or dreaming."

"Believe me Girl, you ain't dreaming! You have me stressed out with all this wedding stuff! When I get married, my man and I are going down to the courthouse and do it quickly and quietly!" Sharon informed her friend.

"You'll think differently about it when it's your turn."

"Oh no I won't! You have done nothing but eat, sleep, and work wedding since Darryl proposed to you. The phone should be surgically attached to your ear!" Dessie and Sharon both laughed picturing what that would look like.

"I can't help it Sharon! Everything that has to be done must be done by phone since I'm here but the wedding is going to be in South Carolina. I'm still waiting to hear from two caterers. It sure doesn't help that I can't get a call at the job without someone finding out my business."

"So now you know that when you tell one lie, it leads into another, and another." Dessie threw Iren's teddy bear at her friend, laughing as Sharon tried to duck the soft blow.

"I wish you would have changed your mind on being my maid of honor. You have been with me through some pretty rough spots, and it would've meant so much to me if you would have stood up with me on that day."

"I'm flattered, but your childhood friend should have that honor. She and you grew up together, and I think that she would've been hurt if you had not offered the honor to her."

"Tash would have been alright with it. She's in medical school right now and that's the only thing that she's thinking of right now."

"I'll tell you what," Sharon said, "if she can't be there for the wedding, then I'll be happy to be there for you."

"Okay, but you do know that I can have two maids of honor don't you?"

"Girl you are too much of a traditionalist for that!" Dessie had to admit that Sharon was telling the truth. Darryl had asked her to move in with him, but she declined saying that it would somehow take away from the magic of the preparation.

"Here Girl, help me find some dresses for the bridesmaids," Dessie said; handing Sharon a couple of bride magazines.

"Girl! How many more of these magazines are you going to buy? You have about thirty of these things already!"

"I know that I have a lot of them, but I want all of us to look good. Plus I want all the bridesmaids in different styles. I know the color that I want, but the styles have to be flattering as well."

"That sounds new and sophisticated. Are they all going to be the same length?"

"I haven't decided on that yet. I'll wait until Debra and Vicki can meet with us and see which ones they like, but I'm going to select at least six of them to choose from. Everybody can have the one they like best. It makes it a lot easier than trying to force somebody to wear something they detest and make them pay for it too!"

"Just how many bridesmaids are you having?"

"With Tasha as my maid of honor, and her little cousin as the flower girl, it'll be five, and I don't have to worry about the little girl's dress.

They are going to get that one down there, and thank God for that! One less thing that I have to deal with!"

"Have you decided what the colors are going to be yet?"

"I'm torn between pastel pink or peach, and I have to make the decision by tomorrow so that I can let the caterers know what colors I'll be using on the tables."

Dessie felt stressed, and it was beginning to show. Trying to stay on top of things was quickly bringing her down. She wished Ruthie were there helping her. She knew all about planning a wedding.

Dessie's greatest fear was having those at work find out about her plans. She was careful not to leave any list, or notes around concerning anything to do with the plans. When she had no choice but to make a phone call concerning it, she went into a conference room.

DC

Darryl's plans weren't half as troublesome as Dessie's were. The major job for him was to find hotel accommodations for family, friends and wedding party members. That was easily accomplished by placing one phone call to the Sheraton Hotel downtown Westfield where he requested ten rooms, and promptly charged them to his MasterCard gold account. Since his father was to be his best man, and two of his attendants would be coming from out of state, all he needed were the measurements from the guys and the tuxedoes would be waiting in the rooms when they arrived. Dessie had asked him to ask Ben to be one of his attendants, and he hadn't gotten around to doing it yet. He promised himself that the next time he saw him, he would ask.

The first time that Dessie entered Darryl's home, she couldn't believe how large and beautiful it was. The place that she and Sharon shared could have fit into his four times. Entering the foyer, you stood under a magnificent chandelier. The floor was just as beautiful in imported Italian tile; bright white with burst of gold throughout it. On her right, just past the foyer, was a sitting room with a fireplace, soft lights and muted green furniture. To the left of the sitting room was

Darryl's study. The walls were lined with bookshelves containing what must have been hundreds of books. Dessie pictured herself doing her own studying in the room. It had everything in it that she would ever need. When Darryl showed her the living room, Dessie almost fainted from its brilliance. The two sofas were all white as were the lamps and chairs. Everything!

"I've never seen a room like this before. It is so beautiful Darryl."

"So you like it?"

"I love it!"

"Well, then it's yours. It was all delivered today. I prayed hard that you would like it."

"I love it, and you too darling! As Darryl pulled her into his arms kissing her passionately, ecstasy overtook them both, and both started to remove their clothing. They didn't bother to go upstairs to one of the four bedrooms. He took her right there on the living room floor. Even with the urgency felt by the two of them, there was none of the awkwardness of school age lovers. Darryl rubbed himself against her without entering her, driving her passions higher than she could have imagined. He was an expert lover, satisfying her completely before climaxing himself deep inside of her.

It seemed like a long time had passed before they broke their embrace. When Darryl rolled off her, she looked straight ahead to a fireplace she hadn't noticed when she first entered the living room. Her eyes slowly went from the bottom of the marble structure to just above the mantle to a portrait of a woman dressed in a beautiful, dazzling white wedding gown standing by a pond with three snow white swans swimming. Dessie jumped up grabbing her clothes hastily. Darryl looked at her surprised by the speed of her gathering her clothing. "What's wrong Honey?" Darryl asked, grabbing his boxers as he stood up. Dessie couldn't say anything, but her gaze remained focused on the portrait. Darryl eyes followed her gaze to where hers already were.

"Oh Honey, I'm so sorry. I intended to move the picture into my study and I completely forgot about it." Dessie was so upset, she wanted to go home. Darryl immediately went over to the portrait and removed it from its place and took it into his study and drew the doors close. Darryl walked back into the living room to find Dessie standing in the same spot he had left her. "I didn't realize that it was there. For the past few months, the lights were never on in here. I'm so sorry." Dessie felt like a villain who had stolen something and was trying to get away as fast as she could. When she saw the look on Darryl's face, she realized that she had overreacted.

"I'm sorry Darryl," Dessie began, "I don't know what came over me. I know that you had a life before we got back together. I just wasn't expecting it in the way that it happened. I don't mean to be selfish, but when I saw the picture, I felt like I was sharing you with her. I don't know if I'm ready to be married to you. I don't think I'm mature enough to love you in the way that I want to." Dessie said, near tears.

"Dessie listen to me; you are who I want to spend the rest of my life with, and this is what Janice wanted me to do. She didn't want me to bury myself in her grave too. Had she been able to, she would have gone out and hand selected the woman that I was to spend the rest of my life with. And you know what?" Darryl asked.

"What?"

"She would have picked you the same way I did long ago." Dessie fell into his arms out of happiness. She thanked God over and over for sending this beautiful man back into her life.

Chapter Nine

Ruthie slowly made her way down to Bea's room. She quietly entered, not knowing if she had a roommate or not. If she did, she wouldn't stay too long. The last time she was in a hospital for any length of time was when Dessie was born. Anything else was handled at home. The curtain had been drawn between the two beds, giving each patient their privacy. Ruthie moved past the curtain where she could see her sister's face. She looked so serene at that moment. She wished that no one would disturb her; just let her rest. She wanted to thank the doctors personally for the wonderful care they had given to her only sibling. Ruthie eased into the chair by Bea's bed. Ruthie noticed that her skin was so clear; she could go out with just a little bit of lipstick on. She cautiously rubbed Bea's hand; marveling at the softness of it. They really had taken care of her. She didn't look sick the way she did the last time Ruthie had seen her. Ruthie didn't believe in a lot of doctor medicine, but it sure did Bea a whole lot of good. She had got her weight back up. She looked like she weighed a good hundred and forty pounds at least. She wondered if the children had been in to see her. Ruthie held her hand for so long; she felt the warmth in it suddenly leave. That's when she broke down and cried heavy sobs of regrets, frustration, sorrows, but most of all, love.

Clanford and Charlene had been sitting outside the room on a small bench when they heard Ruthie break down. Only then did they enter into the reality of what had taken place. Clanford stood behind Ruthie gently but firmly, massaging her heaving shoulders. Clanford didn't rush her; he didn't offer scriptures of comfort. Somehow he knew that that was not what Ruthie needed. She needed to let go of all the years of abuse, crying, praying and humiliation. It was done. Finished.

𝒟𝒞

"Hello? Dessie? Ruthie asked.

"Yeah. It's me Mama. I was just getting ready to call you!" Dessie said excitedly, "I've found the gown that I want you to make!"

"Dessie?"

"Yes Mama?"

"Bea is gone." Ruthie said, but Dessie didn't understand the 'gone' part until Ruthie started sobbing.

"Oh my God! When Mama? How?" Dessie asked all at once.

"She passed this morning. I got there about two minutes before."

"What happened Mama?" Dessie asked, with silent tears coursing down her cheeks.

"She took bad off sick yesterday at the nursing home, and they had a ambulance come and bring her to the hospital. The people at the nursing home said they found three big empty liquor bottles and one half full in her clothes closet. I don't how she got hold of all that liquor, but when I went to get her things, one of those aides told me that some heavyset, dark-skinned woman had started visiting her almost every day for the past three weeks."

"Whoever that was Mama must have been bringing in the alcohol."

"I know child. I know. But it's not going to bring Bea back here. They will have to answer for it in judgment themselves,"

"I'll be there tomorrow Mama to help with the arrangements."

"That would be good Honey. I know that I'm not going to get much help from anybody else."

"Bye Mama. I'll see you tomorrow." Dessie hung up the phone and immediately started getting ready to go home.

DC

Darryl held Dessie in his arms for a long time before she had to go inside the airport. Since security was tight there, it was difficult for non-passengers to gain entrance into airports. Especially in New York.

Once Dessie was seated on the plane, she realized that this was the first time that she was going to be away from Iren for a long period of time. She told Etta that should anything come up concerning the baby, she was to call Darryl and he would contact her. Iren loved being with Etta so much, that sometimes he'd cry when Dessie picked him up from Etta's. He would run and hide under the bed screaming for his 'Nana.' Dessie sometimes had to struggle with him to get him to quiet down. He was awfully strong for a small child. He would probably dominate in his weight class.

DC

Dessie picked up a car at the airport; the one at home probably would not have started, and she knew that she would have to drive her mother around setting up the arrangements.

Driving home, Dessie was amazed at the new changes that had taken place since she had been gone. A super Blockbuster store, an extension added onto the library, and what appeared to be about ten small shops spaced throughout downtown. Just as she was leaving the downtown area, she noticed a catering service called 'Mama's kitchen.' If she had the time, she would stop by before she left town to see what they had to offer for a wedding reception.

When Dessie reached the familiar house, a few cars were parked in front. She pulled into the driveway, and without removing her bags, rushed up the porch steps to the screen door, which was unlatched.

Dessie walked into the living room looking for Ruthie. Not seeing her, she politely said hello to the women sitting there. She assumed that they were from the church. She walked into the kitchen and stood motionless as Ruthie prepared coffee and tea for her visitors. When Ruthie turned around, she almost dropped the tray she was carrying at seeing her child for the first time in over a year. They both cried tears of joy and sorrow. Ruthie couldn't get over how grown up her little girl looked.

"Baby you look so good! That New York must agree with you. You's a full grown woman now!"

"Mama you haven't changed a bit," Dessie said, patting her eyes dry with a napkin. Ruthie stood back and looked at her beautiful daughter.

"Chile, I can't believe that you are about to get married! Seems like yesterday I was scolding you and Tasha about something foolish."

"Believe it Mama. Look at my ring," Dessie said, holding her hand out for Ruthie's inspection. Ruthie marveled at the diamond circled by ten smaller stones.

"Ooh Baby! That man must be a very rich man to give you something like that!" Ruthie said admiringly.

"He's not what you would call rich Mama, but he is very well to do. He's an attorney."

"Is he a Southern boy?" Ruthie asked.

"Sort of. He's from Delaware, but New York is his home now. We met in college years ago." Ruthie hugged Dessie again, and told her to put some pastries on the tray she had set up on the counter, and to bring it into the living room for her.

After Dessie had been introduced to the women from the church, she retreated to the car to get her bags and carried them into her old bedroom. Nothing seemed out of place in spite of the fact that Patrice had occupied it for the last several months.

After Ruthie's company left, Dessie brought up the matter of the arrangements.

"I called the funeral home already. I have to go over there at two to set up the day and time for the service." Ruthie informed her daughter.

"Fuller must be getting rich now. Usually they hold the body for three days just so they can throw in a storage charge before letting you come in to make the arrangements."

"Child, I ain't talking about Fuller! We have a new funeral home here now, and these guys are sharp! They all dress alike, and they have the best manners you've ever seen!"

"Who are they Mama? Where did they come from?" Dessie asked, surprised to hear that there was another funeral home catering to the African American community of Westfield.

"I don't know where they came from, but everybody here seems to be happy about it."

"Where are they located Mama?" Dessie asked.

"On Elizabeth Avenue."

"In Old Westfield?"

"Yeah. They bought one of those old mansions and made it into a funeral home. It's real nice. I went to one of our church members funeral there, and it was so nice and pleasant in there. It felt just like you were sitting in your own living room."

"What is the name of the place Mama?"

"It's called Delaney Brother's Mortuary."

"And what time did you say we had to be there Mama?" Dessie asked, looking at her watch.

"Two o'clock."

"Well Mama, it's about one forty-five now, and if we are going to make it, we have to leave now."

"Well just let me call Reverend C.L. and tell him that you'll take me and he won't have to leave out from the church afterall." Ruthie rushed off to make the call.

DC

"...So Mrs. Harper, you would like to have the services on the day after tomorrow? That's Saturday."

"Yes, I know," Ruthie said, "it'll be better for all those who work and can't afford to take the day off."

"And you want the calling hours to begin at ten and the service to start at twelve noon?"

"That's right." Ruthie told the distinguished man sitting at the head of the conference table.

"And I have her clothing here now," he said as he checked items off on a list. "Would you like to come with me to our casket selection room now?" Mr. Delaney asked, as he had them follow him down a well-lit corridor.

The casket selection room was large with at least fifteen caskets of varying cost and materials. Ruthie selected a simple mahogany half-couch casket with a beige lining and pillow. The total cost for the goods and services purchased, totaled six thousand four hundred and fifty dollars. Dessie instantly reached for her purse. Ruthie stopped her and told her that it was all taken care of. "Mama you shouldn't have to carry the burden of all this by yourself." Dessie pleaded.

"Don't worry about it Dessie," Ruthie said, "I've kept Bea in an insurance policy for the last five years. I knew that this day would come." Dessie cried silent tears for the loss of her aunt, and the foresight of her mother. Ruthie paid the bill on the spot, and with cash.

The morning of the services, someone from the mortuary placed two 'reserved for funeral' cones in front of the house even before Ruthie and Dessie were up. Soon after, people seemed to come from every direction, bringing food and beverages for the repast.

Clanford and Charlene arrived to have prayer before the cortege left for the mortuary. As soon as the prayers were done, they left.

When the limousine pulled into the mortuaries circular driveway, to the entrance, Clanford was standing outside in his pastoral robes; ready to lead the family inside.

Just as everyone was lining up, Dessie saw two figures approaching the crowd. Dessie turned and saw that it was Wesley and Patrice. Both appeared to be wearing clothes that didn't belong to them, or they had lost an awful lot of weight since she had last seen them. Just like Ruthie had told her, Patrice was pregnant, and even an oversized dress couldn't conceal her condition. Patrice noticed Dessie looking back at her, and attempted to hide behind Wesley, but the move was futile since he was smaller than she was. Dessie didn't see either of the boys, but hoped that they would be there to see their mother for the last time.

As the line started to move into the chapel, Dessie could hear Clanford's booming voice reading scripture. She was amazed at its clarity, but saddened by the finality of the words that he read, "I'm the resurrection..."

As soon as they were seated, Boyce and Brent walked into the chapel and took seats alongside Ruthie and Dessie. Patrice and Wesley remained in the rear. Even when the funeral director announced that the final viewing was about to take place, neither bothered to come forth to view the remains.

At the cemetery, Brent lost control of his emotions and allowed his pain and anguish to spill over. Boyce appeared to be angry at the time that it was taking to get Brent back into control, "I told you not to come!" Boyce yelled at his brother, "I got things to do dummy!" Both Ruthie and Dessie looked at each other, and probably had the same thought in their heads. *What's more important than being at your own mother's funeral?*

DC

Ruthie was busy saying goodbye to some of the many church members who had attended the services, as Brent, sitting in Dessie's room, told her of the horrors of the last few months. "At first, they wouldn't let us see them together, but after awhile, they didn't care who saw them. When we got up in the morning, the door to the room would be open and they would be laying in there buck-naked! They both be in there smoking rock all night. All kinds of people be coming to the house to get high and stuff. We always getting up not knowing who in the house. I got up one morning and stepped on this guy sleeping by my bed. Patrice don't know who that baby daddy is. She claim it belong to Wesley, but every time they get into a argument; which is everyday, Wesley tell her that the baby ain't nothing but a trick baby, and that if that baby come out looking white, he gonna put 'em both out on the street. Patrice always tell him that he aint gonna do nothing to her since he the one that put her out there to sell her ass in the first place!"

"What does Boyce have to say about all that's going on?" a shocked Dessie asked.

"He use to be upset at first, but now he don't care since they be giving him rock to get high on. He don't even go to school no more. Most of the time he don't even come into the house; be out hanging with his friends, or doing things that gonna get him some rock. I can't stay in that house no more. I try to buy bread and milk to have something to eat when I come home from school, and it's gone by the time I get home. If the stuff is already been opened, they eat it all up, and if it's brand new, you won't find any of it anywhere. That means that they sold it. We don't have nothing left in the house. Everything we had, Wesley sold it to buy rock, and since Patrice can't go out on the streets like she use to, we really don't have nothing now; but I think she still manage to get out there sometime when Wesley ain't around. Sometimes he don't come home for days and days, and Patrice sit up and cry like a baby over him! I know I can't stay there much longer. I have to go."

"Where are you going to live once you move out of there?" Dessie asked.

"I am going to ask Aunt Ruthie if I can come here and stay with her until I get out of school. That's the only thing I want to do now. Finish school. I had wanted to go to college, but I know that I will never be smart enough to do that."

"If you keep putting yourself down, you will never make anything happen for you, and you are smart enough to go to college!"

"I mean that...well, my record is not all that good. We missed a lot of school, and I usually make it by with C's and D's with a B here and there."

"If you weren't smart, you wouldn't have been able to pass at all because of your high absenteeism," Dessie told a sad looking Brent. "Things are going to work out okay for you Brent. Just keep doing the right thing and you'll see it." Brent smiled for the first time in a long time.

$$\mathcal{DC}$$

"...I like the design baby, but don't you think you'll be showing a little too much skin?"

"Mama, the wedding is going to be in August, and it's so hot here in August. I don't want to wear something that's going to have me sweating profusely."

"But Baby, you barely have enough material covering your front, and you ain't got none at all covering your back."

"It's the style Mama. Everybody that's getting married this year; will be wearing some sort of variation of this gown."

"It's a beautiful dress, but I don't think it's enough of it," Ruthie said, with a heavy sigh, "but if this is what you want, this is what I'll make." Dessie felt a huge sense of relief when she realized that she wasn't going to have to argue with Ruthie over the skimpiness of the gown.

The one thing that she was in favor of was changing the color of the gown from bright white to a shade or two darker; to maybe a slight eggshell.

"I suppose that I could make a veil that's long enough to cover your back. It's cut so low in the back, your panties might slip up and show." Dessie had already thought of the problem and bought the necessary undergarment. Ruthie had to admit that the dress was striking, but she didn't think that the membership of New Holiness was ready for it, and she expressed that concern to Dessie.

"Ma, the dress is so beautiful; I doubt if anyone is going to say anything other than that."

"I can't tell you what to wear, but I wish you would change your mind about this one."

"I have my heart set on wearing this one Mama. I didn't want to wear a veil, but since you say that I'll be showing too much skin, I've decided to let you go ahead and add one."

"Don't worry about having to wear a veil all day. I can make it so that most of it can be removed after the ceremony." The matter was settled and Dessie was free to move on to other things.

She checked her messages back in New York, and found out that both caterers had called her back with the quotes she requested. Instead of calling them back right away, Dessie decided to check out the new catering service that she saw downtown a couple of days earlier.

Ruthie gave Dessie the list of names and addresses so that she could give it to the stationer in New York. She made an appointment to meet with the owners of 'My Mama's Kitchen'. The lady who answered the phone sounded very pleasant.

After tending to all of the things she needed to take care of in Westfield, Dessie needed reassurance from her mother that she would be well in her absence. "Don't worry about me Child. I'll be alright. Brent has started moving his stuff in, and he should be done with that in a day or two. He don't have much."

"But how are you set with money and food Mama?" Dessie asked.

"Child you should know by now that that those two things I don't worry about. As long as I can get somebody to take me to the store every once and awhile, I know we won't starve, and Clanford or Charlene are always nearby."

"Do you think that you might have problems with Brent Mama?"

"Lord no! Brent ain't no trouble all. If that Boyce was here, that would give you something to worry about!"

"Promise me you won't let him move in here too Mama!" Dessie pleaded.

"You don't have to tell me that Dessie Lee! I wasn't going to say anything about this, but about two months back, I had just got back to the house from going grocery shopping when Boyce rang the doorbell. I had just bought a ham and a turkey to fix for the church's 'Feed the Needy' day. Boyce told me that he wanted to go see his mama, but he didn't have any money to catch the bus with. I had a bunch of change on my dresser; so I told him to wait a minute and went to get the change for him. When I got back to the kitchen, Boyce wasn't in there. I figured he changed his mind. I looked out the door and didn't see him; so I went on back to the kitchen to put the food up. I picked up my pocketbook and it was open. I hunted for my change purse and it was gone. I had about sixty-five dollars and some change in it. I know I had it with me when I left the store because I took the receipt from the groceries and folded it up and put it in the change purse with the money." Ruthie strongly confessed.

"Did you ever get the chance to ask him about it Mama?"

"I didn't have to ask him anything! Brent overheard him and Patrice talking about the drugs he got for the money and the ham."

"Ham?" Dessie asked puzzled.

"Yeah. He stole the ham too. I thought that they must have been starving over there, but when Brent told me that they would sell anything and buy drugs with the money, I got mad and told Clanford about it. He told me a few days later that I didn't have to worry about Boyce coming back over here. He must have tried to get in the house cause I saw the paint chipped around the windowsill to my bedroom window. I must have got back to the house sooner than he thought. Clanford done fixed all of that now."

"Do you feel safe here Mama with all this stuff going on?"

"Oh yeah Child! I don't worry about all that's out there in this world. The Lord prepares a way for me somehow. Even before I can see a way, the Lord done already fixed it for me. I just keep holding on to his unchanging hand."

"I just need to know that you are going to be safe here Mama. You shouldn't have to worry about somebody trying to break in here and steal from you, and what if you are right here in the house? They could hurt you or something."

"Dessie, after you have gone through so much, lost so much, and seen so much sorrow and pain, you pretty much don't hold on so tight to this world. Now that Bea's gone on home, its just me now." Dessie didn't like the sound of Ruthie's words, and feared what they would mean.

"Don't tell me that you want to die now Mama?" Dessie half asked and stated.

"Naw child. That ain't it at all. You young folks wouldn't understand what we mean when we say that we don't cling to this world so tight anymore. It don't mean that we want to die or kill ourselves. It just means that we have seen enough till we don't put up that much of a struggle when our time comes." Dessie looked even more confused. "Don't worry about it child. Later on in life, you will see what I mean. No matter how hard I try to 'splain it to you now, you won't know it till you get there."

Dessie really didn't understand what it was that her mother was attempting to teach her, but she suddenly had an overwhelming desire to hold her baby closely and tightly to her. If she could have conveyed these thoughts to Ruthie, she would have heard her mother say now you have started the '*getting ready to leave here mind*.' But she couldn't come out and tell her mother that the journey had already begun.

DC

Dessie met with the owner of the catering establishment, and was quite pleased with the range of services that she could choose from.

The owner, Darlene Grant, was a professional organizer of any event that anyone could think of. It took Darlene about ten minutes to come up with a menu that would please everyone.

Dessie still had not decided on her color scheme for the bridesmaids, but promised to call Darlene as soon as she was back in New York and had decided, along with her friends, what the color of their dresses would be.

Dessie made sure that all was well with Ruthie and Brent before she left; promising to be back a week before the wedding. She needed both of her men badly. Even with the weather being so warm, she felt so cold without them. She booked a return flight for the very next day.

Chapter Ten

Darryl was stretched out on the king-sized bed listening to some mellow jazz tunes. As he listened, he focused on the sound of each instrument individually. First, the tenor sax then the bass. Next, he listened for the sound of the piano and the scratchy sound of the snare drum. When the vocalist started to sing, he could tell that she had her beginning in the church. She had a Nancy Wilson-Billie Holliday like quality to her voice. As he listened to her sing, he imagined her singing with a hundred-voice choir singing behind her. The mind picture was awesome; encompassing all that was within earshot.

He laid back, totally relaxed as his penis seemed to grow to proportions it had never known before. Between the music and the mouth that expertly held him back from spraying over; he could just visualize Dessie working on him in the semi-darkness of their bedroom. He wouldn't want her to make him come this way. He wanted to please her before he lost control of the fire that was building in his loins.

Closing his eyes as the expert lips brought him even closer to the finish line. "Who taught you how to do it like this?" Darryl asked, not expecting a reply to his query. "It's been so long," Darryl moaned out. It was getting intense. He had always known from the first time that he had engaged in sex; that his sex drive was off the chart. What this experienced mouth was doing to him caused him to rise upwards, thrusting his hips in a not too gently way, erupting like a geyser. It was always a copious amount; even when he became aroused twenty minutes later. It was his aim to always satisfy his partner first, then wreak havoc as he got his own, which always pushed his partner into an intense, swirling orgasm. Several women had thanked him for the powerful way he had handled his business. They were forever grateful. He had never met the woman that he could not tame in the bedroom. In his world, she just didn't exist.

Darryl started to drift off into the sweetest sleep as he felt soft hands take hold of his semi-hardness; kissing all around it; pulling and teasing. For some reason, he didn't want to go at it again. It wasn't that he couldn't; he was already hard; he just didn't want to. He turned over on his stomach hoping that the message was getting across. It wasn't. The lips still attempted to garner his attention. They knew that if they did their job just right, compliance would be theirs.

"Damn it Troy! Can't you leave me alone for a few minutes so I can get some rest?" Darryl said, highly annoyed. Feeling hurt, Troy went on the defensive.

"You never seemed to mind in the past when I did my thing back to back on you!" Troy said in a hurt puppy dog way. Troy was a string bean of a guy from Texas. His skin and hair color were exactly the same. At twenty-three, he was blonde before it became vogue.

"I have something to tell you Troy," Darryl said, flipping over on his back, and as an afterthought, covering himself with the bed sheet. "I've met someone very special, and I've asked her to be my wife." Troy sat in shocked silence not knowing what to say or do first. "We won't be getting together anymore after tonight." Tears started to form in the corners of Troy's eyes.

"You knew this when I rang your bell this evening. Why did you let me touch you?" Troy tearfully asked.

"My lady's out of town, and I needed the attention."

"How long have you been seeing this *'lady'* Darryl?"

"A few months, and before you go jumping to conclusions, we've only recently started sleeping together. You knew that this day was going to eventually come."

"How could you do this to me Darryl?" Troy asked in a mournful voice.

"What did you say Troy?" Darryl asked, unbelieving what he had heard.

"*I said*, how could you do this to me when you know that I love you?" Darryl was completely taken aback at the words that Troy had just uttered.

"Where did all of that come from Troy? You and I never agreed on any type of relationship, and *love* most definitely never entered the picture!" Troy buried his face in his hands; weeping bitterly. "Look Troy, I figured you were doing something that you wanted to do. It worked for me because I saw it as a way of taking care of my needs without going out and cheating on my wife with another woman."

"I got news for you Darryl!" Troy said, weeping loudly, "Whomever you fuck when you are married to someone else *is* cheating!"

"Troy man, you keep saying things that I've had no recollection about! When did I ever *fuck* you?" Troy didn't answer him. "It never happened Troy! You invited me to the health club with you. When we got there, I watched you watching me. I gave you the show that you wanted. When you invited me to go with you for a drink at the Shelburne Hotel bar, I knew what was going to happen, but I let you make all the moves. You thought that I was downing all those gin and tonics you kept plying me with. What you didn't know was that when you went to the bathroom, I told the bartender to only bring me water but make it look like the real thing. I only drank water for the duration of the evening." Troy sat in silence as Darryl told him of his so-called seduction. "When I stumbled leaving the bar, I knew that you had already gotten a room for the evening." Troy lowered his eyes remembering how he had undressed Darryl's magnificent body; kissing it in all the right places. "When you started tonguing my balls, I decided to let you go ahead and do your thing. You have a very talented mouth, but I'm sure that you already know that. You got me off twice that night. That alone should have told you that I couldn't have been that high."

"What about all the other times after that?" Troy asked.

"Like I said, you have a talented mouth and you know how to use the fuck out of it!"

"Why did you continue to lead me to believe that you were interested in getting with me and..."

"Hold up Troy!" Barked Darryl, "I didn't lead you into anything! Every encounter we've had, you've initiated it! I just never stopped you."

"Why can't you have us both Darryl?" Troy started to bargain.

"Troy, you are still not listening to me! I'm not gay, and I'm not interested in having a relationship with another man! Now if you don't mind, please leave my home!" Troy stood up and picked his jacket up from the floor and putting it on all the while shedding useless tears.

"I will get you for this Darryl!" Troy told him, in a voice tinged with vengeance.

"And what is that supposed to mean?" Darryl asked, in a laid back way.

"I'm going to make it my business to put the word out at the office that you forced me into a sexual relationship!" Darryl started laughing when he heard Troy's plan. "You won't think that it's so funny when your sorry ass is out of a job!" Troy informed him. "I'm going to the top in the morning and by tomorrow afternoon, you'll be packing your office up!" Darryl got up from the bed still laughing at what Troy had threatened him with.

"In case you haven't heard Troy, another week and a half and my career at Darden and Associates will be over. I've already handed in my resignation." Troy stood there looking dazed by the news. "Telling anybody anything isn't going to do much good!"

"I will file a sexual harassment claim against you!" Threatened Troy.

"Do whatever it is that you think is necessary, but I must warn you that filing such a claim is going to put you in a precarious situation with the firm. They will eat you alive! And you can hang it up if you think that you will leave and go to another firm for an instant job. Law clerks come a dime a dozen! So go ahead! Kill yourself! I think that its time for you to leave!" Darryl led the way to the front door still minus any clothing. Troy could see his ample sex moving between his legs as he followed behind him. "Good night Troy!" Darryl said. Troy looked at him with pleading eyes as Darryl raised a palm letting Troy know that it was over.

"I will ruin you Darryl Matthews! I promise you that I will!" Darryl helped advance Troy's leaving by starting to close the door even before Troy was fully outside; slamming it once he was.

𝒟𝒞

"We don't have to go to some exclusive dress shop to pick out dresses. A lot of outlets carry the same or similar dresses in bulk, and in different styles and colors," Debra informed the group of friends as they sat in the kitchen having a rare, early Saturday breakfast.

"I've selected pink for the color of the accessories for the reception; so if we can find dresses in that color, I won't have to change anything with the caterer," Dessie informed the others, as she struggled to hold onto Iren as she tried to brush his hair. His growth had been amazing. Instead of looking like a one year old, he looked every bit of two going on three! He no longer sucked a bottle; preferred regular food to baby food, and was beginning to be very verbal and understandable. Darryl had him calling him "Da da" as soon as Iren started walking. It got to be a common sight to see Iren sleepily crawl into Darryl's lap when it was time for him to go to bed. Sometimes he would push Dessie to the limit when he wouldn't cooperate with her at bedtime, screaming for his "Da da."

"I think we should go out to Long Island first to look," Vicki suggested. "Parking will be much better out there, plus the prices will be more affordable than those in the city."

"If we go out to the Island, it shouldn't take us all day." Sharon said, hopefully.

"Don't forget that we still have to shop for shoes!" Dessie yelled from the bathroom. The three friends in the kitchen gave each other knowing, tired looks. They knew of the task that was before them.

By six o'clock that evening, four dresses and three pairs of shoes had been bought and paid for. Each dress, the same shade of pink, but uniquely different from each other. All of the bridesmaid's dresses were short. The maid of honor's dress was an off the shoulder, tea length, elegantly designed dress that would look lovely on Tasha's lithe frame. Dessie was going to send it to her immediately so that if any alterations were needed, she could have them done before the wedding.

Vickie and Sharon's dresses were similar in style except Sharon's was cut lower in the front and Vickie's was lower in the back. Debra's dress had the fuller skirt with spaghetti straps and a totally sheer pink coat over the dress trimmed in pink satin. All three looked fantastic in their ensembles. A major area of the wedding was now taken care of.

DC

Between work, school, and Iren, Dessie had had little time for the man in her life. If they managed to talk on the phone on more than three occasions in one week, it was a rare thing. Seeing each other called for strategic planning.

After a few frustrating tries, Dessie was tempted to take Darryl up on his earlier offer of moving in with him, but she still wanted to hold on to some of the traditional values of courtship and marriage. Darryl had teased her about being so "traditional" when they first reunited.

"I knew that you were lying about being married the first time we saw each other again."

"How did you know that? Was it in my voice?" she asked.

"Well, that too, but the one thing that let me know that you weren't, was the fact that you weren't wearing a wedding band, and you are way too much of a traditionalist to ignore that fact." Dessie was so embarrassed about the deceit that she tried to pull off, till she sometimes thought that everyone knew her secret; they were just too polite to tell her.

Darryl almost had her ready to move in when he planned a romantic evening for just the two of them beginning with chilled glasses of wine followed by a dinner of grilled steaks, baked potatoes, and a tossed green salad. After they had dined, Darryl escorted Dessie upstairs to the master bathroom; that was as big as a small bedroom. The main attraction was the huge, round whirlpool bathtub with pulsating jets of water all alongside its interior surface. The walls were covered with a paper print of bulrushes in muted grey, beige and white. The room was lit by track lighting around its circumference. The tub itself was soft beige. Darryl turned on the water jets, and the tub filled in seconds. "Well, are you going to stand there, or are you going to join me?" Darryl asked Dessie, as he started to disrobe. Seeing his muscular naked frame was all the convincing she needed.

"I wouldn't miss this moment for anything!" she said, as she started undressing, and watching him become aroused.

Darryl had the complete set of Sea of Tranquility Body Works, and the fragrance had transformed the bath into a luxury spa without the expense or the time limit. Darryl adjusted some buttons on the tub and the lights dimmed and music started playing all around them. Dessie laid her head on his chest and drifted into the lushness of the moment. Getting into the music, Dessie sat up when she recognized the song that was playing. Her eyes misted as she looked into his before searching out his lips and kissing them passionately. The music that was playing was Quincy Jones, the one that he was playing when he first laid eyes on her.

Dessie walked into the office the next morning feeling more relaxed and stress free than she had in months. For once she felt that she could handle everything that came her way. But she wasn't prepared for the shock she was about to receive. Everyone was speaking in hushed tones. The office seemed to be quieter than usual. Dessie walked into her small office and picked up a memo on her desk. She was shocked into silence by its message. Attorney Mortson had been struck and killed as he walked along the Long Island Expressway this morning.

The memo went on to say that it looked as if he intentionally had walked into the path of the car that struck him; throwing him into the path of a tractor-trailer that drove over his body. It appeared that it was a deliberate act since his car was found less than a half-mile from where he was hit with its engine running. Harry had never gotten over the death of his soul mate Tillie, and decided to end his life in the same manner. It felt downright eerie. How could anyone have known that his depression had taken away his will to live? The funeral would be in the morning at nine a.m. at the Riverside Mortuary on 49th Street. The memo went on to say that the firm would be closed the next day in observance.

Some of the partners openly mourned Harry's death. Others acted as if nothing out of the ordinary had occurred. As the day wore on, it became clear how well respected and loved Attorney Mortson was to so many people. Notes of condolences seemed to continue arriving long after lunch, and into the early evening hours.

Dessie called her contacts at the deli, and informed them of what the firm would need, and where to have the goods delivered. Before she left for the day, she set up the coffee service and all of the utensils needed. She had been informed to keep everything simple and subdued.

After the service, Dessie went straight to the office to make sure that everything was in place to receive the guest; who would start arriving as soon as they left the cemetery.

About a hundred people showed up at the office. Once everything was set into motion, Dessie retreated to her office to get schedules back together, and to rearrange appointments that had to be cancelled due to the tragedy. As she worked, Dessie thought to herself that Tillie and

Harry had had such a special love and attachment to each other; that the outcome would have been the same regardless of the circumstances. Neither could have sustained themselves in this world alone. A broken heart was just taking too long to end his suffering.

DC

"She had a girl early this morning," Ruthie told Dessie.

"I can't say that I'm overjoyed by the news Mama."

"Dessie, whenever the Lord gives us another life, we have to embrace and love that life. This child is going to need a lot of love and prayers just to keep her here. She barely weighs two pounds. The doctors are working on her around the clock." Dessie felt for the child after Ruthie said that, but she refused to feel anything for Patrice for the damage that she has caused this child to suffer.

"Well, how is Patrice doing Mama?"

"She okay, but the doctor says that she is seriously undernourished and need medical care herself."

"Mama, I can hear it in your voice," Dessie started saying, "You are in no position to deal with Patrice and all of her problems. She has Wesley and Boyce there to help her out."

"Child, Boyce been locked up for the past month for breaking into somebody's house over on the west end of town."

"He'd better be careful Mama. Even though things have changed a lot in the South, some people still harbor old prejudices."

"He called me asking me if I could come and get him out of jail. I told him that I didn't have any money for that, and he just hung up the phone without even saying goodbye. He might not understand the reason why I told him 'no' right now, but if he keeps living, he might realize that I was trying to save his life."

Dessie realized that the problems that her cousins were bringing on themselves were starting to affect the whole family, and it made Dessie fearful for her mother's well being.

"Mama, if you have any notions about letting Patrice come and stay there again, you should reconsider and realize that you are not helping them. You are only making it easier for them to continue living the way that they have been." Ruthie sighed heavily, and wished that life had been different for her nephews and only niece.

"I suppose you are right Child. It don't look like nothing I did over the years have made any difference to them."

"You can't blame yourself for that Mama," Dessie said in a sensitive tone. "Aunt Beatrice set the tone for everything that went on in their lives."

"I know, but I just feel so bad about everything."

"You shouldn't. You did more than anybody else would have done. The next time Patrice calls you about coming there to stay, tell her to call social services, or the nearest women and children's shelter. They are better equipped than you are to see that she and her baby are well cared for. "How is my gown coming along Mama?" Dessie asked, abruptly changing the subject.

"Oh Honey! It is a beauty! I'm almost finished with it. The bodice is the heaviest part of it. It took me hours to get it where I wanted it. I sewed the whole thing by hand including the lining. I just need you to try it on once you get here, and then I could put in the permanent stitches. I turned down four or five sewing jobs just so I could get your gown done."

Ruthie didn't know it, but Dessie was silently crying on the other end of the line, and she really didn't know why. She didn't know if it was the way her mother described the beauty of the dress, or for giving her mother the opportunity to give her little girl a beautiful wedding.

"Oh, before I forget Mama, take Brent's measurements for me. He can be an usher at the wedding. I don't want him to feel left out."

"That's a good idea Dessie. He sure has been a big help to me since he been here."

"I'm so glad to hear that Mama. At least one of them appreciates you. I have to go and get ready for work Mama, and besides, we've been on this phone for so long, your phone bill is going to be sky high!"

"I don't care about no bill Child!" They always get paid don't they? But you go ahead and get ready for your job, and I will talk to you later."

"Bye Mama."

Chapter Eleven

As the date of her departure neared, Dessie clung to Iren; knowing that she would not see her beautiful son for close to three weeks. Even the thought of leaving him hurt. She wasn't concerned about his well being, she was just going to miss him so much.

Dessie played a game with Iren where she made believe that she was crying, and he would come and tenderly pat her on the head, plant wet kisses on her cheeks to placate her. If she carried the game on too long, Iren would start to whimper himself, and Dessie would cuddle and tickle him till he laughed with joy.

𝒟𝒞

Darryl removed the last of his belongings from the middle drawer of his desk. He came across a slip of paper with Troy's name, address, and phone number on it. Looking at it, he remembered when Troy gave it to him.

Darryl was at the office late working on a couple of pro bono cases. Mr. Darden detested the work, but he allowed the attorneys that worked for him to do them because they helped to sharpen the skills of less seasoned attorneys. His only requirement was that they had to use their own time to work on them. He was sitting at his desk concentrating on the work in front of him when someone knocked on his office door. "Come on in," Darryl said to the unknown visitor.

When the door opened, Troy was standing there in what he must have thought was a provocative stance.

"How are you doing Darryl? Why are you still here working so late?"

"Working late doesn't bother me. I have a deadline to meet or my client will forfeit a large sum of money."

"I know what else is large, and I would love to help you work on that!" Darryl felt a familiar stirring as he thought about what Troy's talented tongue and mouth had done to him. Darryl pushed himself away from his desk and spun his chair around so that he was no longer facing his desk. He leaned way back into the soft, plush leather chair. That was all the invitation Troy needed. He was on his knees in a flash; frantically trying to get Darryl's pants below his waist. Accomplishing that, he proceeds to take him on a journey to a thousand places he had never been before. This was not his first experience with oral sex, but it felt as if it was.

"If you could put that in a bottle and sell it..." Darryl said out loud. Troy couldn't respond; his mouth was full.

After he was finished, Troy stood up and leaned over Darryl's chair and gave him a hug and lightly kissed his ear. Darryl jumped from the contact. Troy took it as if it was the aftershock of a tremendous orgasm, but Darryl's thoughts were on *I'm not kissing a man!* Before he left, Troy wrote down his address and phone number and gave it to Darryl. Darryl looked at it; knowing that he would never call the number on it.

Darryl tore the slip of paper into so many pieces, it would be impossible for anyone to ever discover what was written on it.

It felt good to be packing up and leaving. It had been a rough year for him, but now that he was financially secure, he could afford to explore the many options presented to him. Five months prior, he had met with two brothers that had gone to Yale at the same time he had, and wanted to head up their own law firm. All three needed financial backing, and opening up in debt up to their necks didn't appeal to the three. When Janice died, Darryl collected over five hundred thousand dollars in insurance benefits. Once he had the needed capital, the decision to move ahead was simple. And what he liked even more was the fact that he would own more of the firm than the other two investors. He was watching his dream materialize right before his eyes.

The house that Janice's parents had given them as a wedding gift, was his to keep as long as he lived in it. It was paid for so he didn't have to worry about a mortgage; just keep the yearly taxes paid on the property. The only time that Janice's parents had been at the house was for their daughter's memorial service. That's when they had told him to keep the place. They knew that they wouldn't be coming back to New York to live. The only stipulation that they had concerning the house, was that he could not sell it and pocket the proceeds. The money would come to them, or Janice's two remaining siblings.

Dessie would be moving in shortly. The wedding was coming closer, and they wanted everything in place by the time they returned from their honeymoon. Dessie begged Darryl to tell her where they were going, but he wouldn't budge an inch.

Darryl could hardly believe his luck. Last year at this same time, he was grieving the fate of his wonderful, unselfish bride. Her courage and optimism was the only thing he seemed to survive on. Even when the doctors had told them that there was no hope of her ever recovering, she still wouldn't give up on herself. It taught him a lot about the human spirit. Seeing her trying to fight the thing that was weakening her body, often sent him off to be by himself where he wouldn't have to check his tears. She told him that the day was going to come when he could smile again, and she was right. His life was filled with a new awareness of all that surrounded him. A chance meeting opened the door to a great beginning. He was thankful that Dessie had decided to give them another chance. He was going to show her that she hadn't made a mistake.

DC

A week before the wedding, Dessie was busy packing everything that she would need for the next two weeks. She wasn't having much luck with the chore. Things that she needed for home, she wouldn't need on her honeymoon, and vice versa. She was about to throw her hands up in despair when she thought of her old roommate and her method for getting things back and forth during the school year. She would mail her trousseau home, and travel with her everyday clothes.

Iren was sleeping in his crib after a fussier than usual afternoon. It was almost as if he knew that his mommy was about to leave him. Dessie looked on his beautiful sleeping face, and automatically started stroking his large black curls. Dessie wished that she could take him with her to show him off to all she knew.

Dessie wondered if she would see Ray when she arrived home. She wasn't expecting to though. She had gone through great pains to have the wedding downtown at the Christian Life Center instead of New Holiness. She didn't want to be surprised by him showing up. Ruthie was a little bit upset by her daughter's decision, but she understood the reason behind it. But had Dessie consulted her, she would have told her that Ray rarely made an appearance at church these days.

DC

On the night before Dessie was to leave for home, Sharon burst into her bedroom glowing. "You will never guess what happened tonight!" Sharon said, on the verge of tears. "Ben proposed to me tonight! Look!" she said, as she held her hand out to show Dessie the diamond that Ben had placed on her finger. "He was so sweet when he asked me to marry him!"

"How did he do it? What did he say?" Dessie asked excitedly.

"First, he asked me did I have any idea as to where our relationship was going."

"And what did you say?"

"I asked him where did he want it to go, and he said that he was tired of living alone, going to bed alone. I need... I said hold up a minute buddy! I don't have any intention of shacking up with anybody! And if you are tired of going to bed alone, I suggest you get a teddy bear to keep you company! I told him that he must be out of his mind if he thought that I was going to move him in with me just because you were moving out!"

"Now why did you have to throw me in the mix?" Dessie laughingly asked.

"Wait a minute Girl! Let me finish! We were just sitting there in the car not saying anything to each other, when he put his arm around me and I relaxed a little, and only a little! I was still ready to let him know that I wasn't about to let him play me. The minute I started to tell him that his charm wasn't going to work, the arm that he had around my neck started moving up and down. It took me a second to see that what he had in his hand was a diamond ring. I couldn't open my mouth. I started crying. I felt so bad for the way that I had yelled at him."

"What's to feel bad about? Its just what he wanted!" Dessie rationalized. "Now I can help you with your wedding. I'll be an expert at it after next weekend!"

"Oh no honey! We are not going that route! I want a simple ceremony with just my family and a few friends."

"You mean to tell me that you don't want to go through all this fun stuff that I'm going through right now?" Dessie said, with a fake exasperated look on her face.

"Girl, the money that we would spend on some big fancy wedding, we could put a down payment on a nice home."

"Leave it to you Sharon to think logically about everything. Just think, tonight is our last night as roommates. We won't have a chance to be there for each other as often as we have been." Dessie said sadly.

"Don't say that Dess! We are still going to be close."

"Somehow it won't be the same."

"It's going to be better!" Sharon said. "We'll be two old married ladies calling each other to complain about how our husbands are always working and never home!"

"I better not have to make a call like that! If Darryl isn't home, then I'd better be with him!"

"I hear you girl! Keep that brother in check!"

Dessie and Sharon spent the rest of the night talking and planning their futures. Early the next morning, Dessie delivered Iren to Etta to care for until she returned. Before she left for the airport, Darryl and she moved the remainder of her belongings to what would be her new home. *Their* new home.

𝓓𝓒

"It's me Mama! I made it in!" Dessie said loudly, as she walked into the house through an unlatched screen door. After calling out for her mother a second time, Dessie's heart started to beat faster as she looked in every room and her mother weren't in any of them. Dessie went to the back of the house, and there was her mother; sitting under the old pecan tree, in perfect shade, churning away on her old ice cream maker. Dessie smiled with relief finding her mother toiling as she'd always done. "Hi Mama!" Dessie said, once she was close enough to be heard.

"Oh child you scared me!" Ruthie said, standing up to give Dessie a hug, and sitting back down to the old fashioned churn.

"Mama, why don't you let me get you one of those new, electric ice cream machines? You use your own recipe, but you don't have to put in all this labor. Some of them even work right in your own refrigerator."

"Or I could just get Brent or Reverend C.L. to run me over cross town to Winn Dixie, and I can just buy me a couple of those already made gallons." Ruthie said, smiling up at Dessie as her arm made small work of her task.

"You won't ever change, will you, Ruth Ann Harper?"

"Everybody that I know of, who made a change for the better, but for what I call it, 'the easier,' ain't lived too long past them making that decision. So if working a little harder, and doing things on my own gives me a little more time, then I'd better keep at it!" Ruthie said, laughing at herself as she picked up the pace on the churn.

"How has everything been around here since the last time I was home Mama?"

"Everything has been pretty much the same. The biggest news that went around for a week or two last month was Thomas and his wife having three babies in one day."

"*Thomas*? *Three babies*? Thomas who Mama?" Dessie asked, puzzled as to whom she was talking about.

"Thomas!" Ruthie said. "Tasha's brother Thomas. He and his wife had three babies at once. Tasha was here for three or four days last month. I thought she would have told you."

"We don't get a chance to talk that much anymore since she's in medical school now."

"Well, don't worry about it. I saved the newspaper with the pictures on the front and everything."

"They had their pictures on the front page?" Dessie asked, with a look of utter shock on her face.

"Oh yeah! Birdie and James would have gone down to that newspaper place, and one way or another, some of them were going to be on that front page!" Ruthie's tone let Dessie know that the Wright's were not going to let this big event go unnoticed. "Child, you should see them! They are the three tiniest, little chocolate kisses you've ever seen! Don't ask what theys names is, cause I can't tell you. These young folks these days, names they children names so that only they can call 'em. Anybody try to kidnap 'em, they'd have to give 'em back cause they can't spell the doggone names; can't say 'em either! I hope that when you start to have children Dessie, you don't go outta your head naming them names that sound like cuss words to me!" Dessie saw this as the best possible time to tell her about Iren.

"Mama I..." Dessie's voice trailed off as a blank look crossed her face.

"What is it Dessie?"

"I...I was just going to ask you were they boys or girls Mama?"

"Two boys and a girl. She was the smallest of the three. The boys look just alike. I don't know how to tell those two apart. I was going down to Birdie's every day when they first came home to help out."

"Do Thomas and his wife live with Mr. and Mrs. Wright now?" Dessie asked.

"Naw. They was just staying down there for a little while till she was able to handle the babies by herself in the daytime. I know what its like to take care of one baby, but three at a time, now that's a job!" Ruthie unclamped the arm of the churn, and lifted the bucket out and headed towards the house. "I been wondering about putting a strip of caramel through this vanilla, but I don't know if I'm going to serve peach cobbler or berry pie for dessert after the rehearsal."

"Do the peach cobbler Mama."

"I knew you were gonna say that Dessie Lee! If you could have peach cobbler for breakfast every day, you'll have it! You gonna watch this caramel and let me know when its ready."

"I don't mind Mama. I don't mind at all." Dessie said, as she washed her hands at the sink.

DC

"Ooo Baby you look so good! I wish Desmond was here to see his little girl!"

"You know Mama, I believe he is here, and have always been. I believe Daddy watches over us. It's every little girl's dream to have her father walk her down the aisle on the biggest day of her life. With Clanford giving me away, it's like...somehow, Daddy is too, and I know he's not going to miss my wedding."

uthie had tears in her eyes as she looked on her daughter. The veil that she had fashioned to compliment Dessie's gown, was a small ring held in place with two hairpins, and the bride's own hair. Ruthie wasn't sure if Dessie was going to have enough hair for the ring or not since Dessie frequently changed hairstyles. Ruthie had left spaces on the ring where she could add flowers if Dessie wanted them. If not, she had enough material to completely cover the ring. The veil itself, were actually three separate pieces that were tied onto the ring beginning with the longest and widest piece of material first. The second piece is added, and then the third and sheerest piece last. The effect was breathtaking, and added charm without being ostentatious.

Ruthie had worried that with all the netting she had to use, the veil would pull her head backwards; making her eyes appear wide and slanted. Thanking God that all had gone well so far, Ruthie hoped that she would have the same luck with the dress. Finding everything in the exact same shade of off white, at the very least, was a doubting task in itself. All she had to do to the dress was to put in the hem in it. It was meant to be long and flowing, so Ruthie had left extra fabric on it until Dessie came with her shoes and she could do the final measuring. She wanted to take care of the matter right then and there, but Dessie begged off; saying she was tired, and that she still had to go into town to set some appointments for her friends.

Dessie wasn't sure if her friends would want to visit Shear Energy, but she felt comfortable setting up the appointments. She knew how much they liked being pampered, and even if they only opted for manicures or pedicures, the appointments would be set. Dessie decided to set one for Ruthie as well. She was determined to get Ruthie to let someone else pamper her for once. She was not going to accept no for an answer.

Dessie drove around aimlessly after setting up the appointments at the salon. Before she knew it, she was in front of her old job. Suddenly, she felt as if she was watching a movie. A young woman exited the building laughing; followed by a man who was also laughing as they walked towards some cars. Dessie couldn't believe her eyes. It was Ray! Her hands trembled on the steering wheel. She watched as Ray placed his hand on her lower back, and opened the car door for the young woman to get in. She wanted to scream to the woman to run as fast as she could to get away from him! Dessie watched as they pulled out of the parking lot. She thanked her lucky stars that the car she had rented had tinted glass, and it was almost impossible for anyone to see inside. She sat in the car for at least ten minutes. She waited because she didn't want to chance an encounter. They looked as if they were headed out to lunch, but Dessie, knowing Ray; it was probably a sex break.

Dessie drove back to her mother's where she knew that she would be safe. She didn't understand why his presence affected her in this way. She didn't feel any love for him. In fact, she looked at him as a nothing.

Ruthie could tell just by looking at her daughter that something was wrong, and she more or less knew who it was that caused her to feel that way. "You went to see that man didn't you gal?" Dessie was silent and adverted her eyes away from Ruthie's steady gaze.

"I didn't go to see him Mama. I accidentally came into contact with him. He didn't see me, but I saw him and the young woman he was with."

"Does that bother you Dessie?" Ruthie asked.

"Does what bother me Mama?"

"Does seeing him still conjure up feelings inside you?"

"It brings up something in me, but it sure isn't anything good!" Ruthie seemed to be holding her breath as Dessie spoke. "I could almost feel the deceit that he was laying on that young girl. I wish I could prevent her from making a fool of herself."

"It wouldn't do any good Dessie. I tried to warn you didn't I?"

"I suppose you're right Mama. The man and the trash that he was feeding me blinded me. I wish that I had never been so stupid."

"Just thank the good Lord above for allowing you to wake up and see where you were heading. Let me tell you something that my Mama told me a long time ago; she told me that the two biggest drunks in town was a man and a woman. She said that every Saturday night, she and about five other men would go out into the woods and sit around a old still that one of 'em had made, and they would drink that moonshine 'til they couldn't drink no mo! By the time they made it back to town, they's was falling and flipping down all over the place. Usually where the flopped at last is where they stayed until the next morning. Now the funny side of this whole thing, from what my Mama told me, is how the folks treated the woman. You could go to any store, church, gas station, anywhere! And ask them the name of one of the men that was out on the town getting drunk with that woman and they couldn't tell you. But ask them who was that woman, and everybody knew her name! The moral of the story is this: you are never going to be able to do what a man can do. I don't mean that you can't hold a job like a man, or fly a airplane like I see women doing now, but if you had did what that man did to you, never having no intention on marrying you, folks would still be talking about you right now. Women are always hollering about equal rights and stuff, but I don't know of one woman who wants to walk around here and have the kind of reputation that some mens have. Some of those same drunk men could have got up and went to church and nothing at all would have been said against them. Not that woman! Every Sister, Missionary, Deacon, and Preacher would turn his or her noses up at her and treat her like garbage! What I'm trying to say to you is that no matter what you do in this world, because you are a woman, people will remember it. Just thank God that you weren't married to that man! What he did with you, he'll do with somebody else."

Dessie knew that what her mother was saying was the truth. She had thought that when she had returned to the house, she would tell her mother about Iren. She couldn't do it now. It would have to wait. "And Dessie Lee," Ruthie began, "whatever you did here, you leave it buried here. Don't go taking all this old mess back up there with you and your new husband. Everybody makes mistakes. You ain't the first and you won't be the last. You can't go through life beating yourself to death because of a mistake that you made. We are all human, and humans are not machines. Even a machine breaks down sometimes and need a wise human touch to get back in shape. Let the past go! You won't be happy with your husband to be, and he sounds like a person who deserves to find some happiness in his life. You should be the one that brings him that happiness."

Dessie felt relieved and sad at the same time. Without condemning her, Ruthie instructed her to let the past remain where it was, and sad because she was unable to reveal the result of her failed romance.

"You haven't tried on your gown yet Dessie, and I need to put the finishing touches on it." Dessie was happy for the respite. She didn't want to think any more. She didn't want to listen any more.

DC

"Mama, where is Brent? I haven't seen him since I got here this morning."

"Hold still now before I stick you. Brent is doing fine. He has done so well in school that his counselor called to tell me that if he keeps on working the way he's been doing, he can probably graduate on time, and Child! That boy can sho nuff sing! Every Sunday he leads that choir like he was born singing! When that child sings 'How Great Thou Art,' there's not a dry eye in the house! When I asked him who taught him to sing like that, he said he didn't know, and that's the way he has always sang. You should have him sing at the wedding. Turn around so I can pin the back."

"Darryl is having a soloist flown in to sing at the ceremony Mama."

"Well, maybe he can sing a song at the reception, you think?"

"Sure. That would be okay Mama," Dessie said in a distracted tone.

"Step down and walk over to the mirror." Ruthie instructed. Dessie did as she was told, and gasped when she saw her reflection in the full-length mirror. The gown was made of off white duchess satin; a very fine piece of material. The bodice was crystal beaded by hand with a low cut back with a hidden zipper. It was an exquisite creation. Ruthie had Dessie try on the veils again to see the total effect. Everything matched perfectly. Dessie opted not to wear a veil over her face, but even that did not take away from the demureness Dessie felt that she had to portray. Ruthie cried as she watched her little girl transform into an elegant, mature woman.

"Why are you crying Mama?" Dessie asked soothingly.

"I just wish that Desmond was here to see you looking so beautiful!"

"You know Mama," Dessie said, "as long as we still love those that are gone, they are still with us, and nothing can separate us from their love. Not even death Mama."

DC

It was two days later when Dessie met up with Brent. Dessie seemed to have something to do everyday that took her away from the house. When she would call Etta, she did so outside of the house. She didn't want to chance being overheard by Ruthie.

Dessie had just gotten out of bed, and was headed to the bathroom when she heard the sweet, melodious lyrics of Luther's *"A House Is Not A Home."* She thought that it was strange of Ruthie to be listening to a rhythm and blues station when it was known that she kept the radio locked on the local Christian station. Dessie stuck her head into the kitchen where Brent, with his back to her, was buttering some toast and tearing Luther up! Ripple and all! From low to high, his range was incredible! As soon as he turned around and saw Dessie, he stopped and turned into his old self. "Hey Cuz! What's up?" he asked.

"You are!" Dessie said excitedly. "Who taught you how to throw down like that?"

When were younger, me and Boyce would always listen to the radio at night, and we'd say that one day we were going to make records and get rich! We were just talking. We were never really serious about it.

Then when Boyce started getting high and stuff, we stopped singing to each other at night."

"Are you telling me that Boyce can sing like you also?" Dessie asked, almost mesmerized by Brent's words.

"I know that he *use* to be able to sing like me, but since he started messing with drugs, he don't sing anymore. I don't think he has any dreams anymore."

"This is absolutely amazing! You guys actually learned how to sing from listening to the radio!"

"Yep. Ma would put us to bed and leave the radio playing. We learned every song, every commercial that came on. It was our babysitter."

"You keep yourself clear of trouble, go to school, and I know that you can make it beyond your wildest imagination!"

"Oh I'll keep out of trouble, but I don't want to make my living singing!"

"But why not? You have a wonderful voice."

"I just like to sing for fun. I really want to make it in the Olympics."

"You can still do both!" Dessie said loudly, as Brent rushed out to catch his bus to the mall. It was great to see Brent doing so well for himself. A stable home life has worked its nurturing charm.

Ruthie heard Dessie moving about in the kitchen, and went in there to talk to her. "The hospital called this morning Dessie."

Dessie's heart started to beat wildly, expecting to hear that something had happened to Iren or Darryl. "They said that Patrice hasn't been there in the last two or three weeks to check on the baby. They want to know do she plan on keeping the baby, or put her up for adoption."

"Maybe that's what she should do Mama."

"Oh Dessie Lee! Don't go talking that old foolish talk! We don't go giving our babies up like that!"

"I didn't mean it the way it sounded Mama. I meant it in a good way. As long as Patrice is out on the street getting high, she doesn't need to have the child with her. The baby would be better off in foster care."

"If the social worker can get in touch with Patrice, they gonna ask her to give the baby up. I need you to take me over there where they live at to let her know that these people are trying to get in touch with her."

"I'll do that Mama, but I have to run over to the caterer's to pay the final bill for the reception, and I'll be right back for you. Is that okay with you Mama?"

"Yes Dessie. That will be fine."

DC

Dessie desperately needed to get out of the house as soon as she could. When Ruthie had come into the kitchen, she could barely keep her hands from shaking. It wasn't that she didn't feel for her cousin's plight; it was just so hard for her to understand how a person who didn't have very much to begin with, could take what little that they did have and squander it on drugs. She believed that there were always choices that a person could choose from. She thought of Brent and how he saw himself in a bad situation and decided to try to pull himself away from it, and it worked. She felt his pain and loneliness when he spoke about his twin and how they use to sing to each other for comfort and hope of a better life. Why his brother and sister couldn't manage to maintain hope for a better life was a puzzlement to Dessie. Hadn't they already seen enough of pain in their brother and mother's life? It did make her angry that Patrice was willing to bring a life into the world, but not willing to be responsible for the life of that child.

It also made her angry that her mother was the only one that came to the aid of her cousins and whatever predicament they happened to find themselves in. Why don't they run to the drug dealers that they give all their money and possessions to? Those are the people that should help out! But when it all comes down to it, nobody makes you take the drugs; it was the individual's choice! Dessie promised herself that she was going to make sure that her children knew how to make safe choices for their lives. She was not going to leave them alone to fend for themselves, or leave them in the hands of people that will do nothing but exploit them for their own selfish reasons. She wouldn't be able to account for them if God saw fit to take her away from them before they became mature adults, but she would form the type of bond with whatever family and friends she had remaining to continue to raise her children with the same moral fortitude that she would want them to possess. She knew without a doubt that Darryl would want it that way too.

Chapter Twelve

"What are you doing here Troy? I thought that I had made myself clear. You are not wanted here!"

"I needed to see you Darryl. I didn't think that you would mind. I'm not interrupting anything am I?"

"Whether you were or not, I meant what I said about you not coming back around. Do I need to get a restraining order to put a stop to this?"

"Do you really want to go that public about our relationship Darryl? What do you think your pretty little wife-to-be would have to say about this?" Troy asked, with a half smile playing at the corners of his mouth; giving Darryl the impression that he knew more than what he was telling. Darryl could see Dessie walking out on him if any details of what occurred between Troy and he ever slipped out. Darryl had to think fast, *and* correctly.

"What do you want from me Troy?"

"I want you Darryl. Since the first time we got together, you've been in my head and heart."

"Troy, we've gone over this issue longer than we should have. When I asked you what you wanted from me to end this confusion, I meant money, a car, vacation...something like that." Darryl's mind was in overdrive. He had to nip this in the bud before it ruined everything he was trying to accomplish. If his partners found out about his

172

involvement with Troy, it could sour the relationship between them. Troy stood just inside the vestibule appearing to be in deep thought. "Look, why don't you think about it, and we can meet later to discuss it." Darryl kept looking behind him as if he was afraid that someone was going to sneak up behind him.

"Why can't I just meet you here Darryl? It'll be easier for me." Darryl gave him a look that indicated that he was not alone without actually saying it.

"I feel you," Troy said in response to the look.

"Why don't we meet at the Shark Bar on Amsterdam tonight at eight? We could get something to eat, and maybe have a few drinks." Troy eyes brightened when Darryl mentioned drinks. He felt that if Darryl drank, he would be more receptive to his suggestions.

"I'll see you at eight then," Troy said, as he sort of bounced down the steps.

Darryl had to work fast. He didn't have a whole lot of time, but he had to close Troy's mouth once and for all. He couldn't give him the opportunity to ruin his life. It was easier to silence him now than to wait until he was in the public's view and not be able to control what he would say or do.

Darryl retreated to his study where he kept a record of every case that he had worked on. He recalled working on a case that involved a murder and drugs, and a huge sum of money. The guy walked away with a slap on the wrist along with a small fine. Darryl remembered going into the courthouse restroom and puking until he had the dry heaves.

When he walked out of the courthouse that dark and dreary day, the defendant and two members of his posse approached him, and thrust a leather briefcase into his unwilling hand.

"This is just a little something to say 'thanks for looking out.' My number is in the bag. Should you ever need anything...anything at all, you let me know and I guarantee that it'll be done. It's not a maybe or a perhaps; it's done!" The three were gone as soon as they had appeared.

Darryl didn't ever think that he would ever need the likes of them, but the situation that he was now faced with, demanded swift action. He located the card and dialed the number.

DC

"I wish there was something we could do Mama, but there isn't. Patrice did not want to give the baby up for adoption, but she was nowhere near to being able to care for a newborn." Dessie said to her mother. When Ruthie walked into the house, she knew that there was no food in there without even looking. Ruthie said that there was a man and a woman sleeping on the bare living room floor. After Ruthie had delivered the message that the hospital had sent, she came and got back in the car. Patrice followed her out and stood on the porch with her hands on her hips and a cigarette hanging from her lips. Dessie blew the car horn and waved at Patrice. Patrice gave her a cold, hard stare and flicked what was left of the cigarette in her direction, and turned and went back into the house without closing the door behind her.

Dessie was surprised at her coolness at first, but decided that it probably appeared to Patrice as if Dessie had it all, but if only she knew the truth! She would realize that they had a lot more in common than just kinship. Dessie informed Ruthie of all that she had learned on babies born to crack addicted mothers. She hoped that it would help her decide to not get involved with Patrice's problems. Ruthie listened to what Dessie had to say. It did make a lot of sense to her, and she knew that taking care of a baby that small was a big undertaking.

Dessie arranged to pick up Tasha from the airport. She had found out from Tasha's mother what time her flight would arrive, and told her that she would love to surprise her since it had been quite a long time since the two had seen each other.

Dessie located the gate that Tasha would be coming through, and sat with oversized sunglasses on, waiting for her friend's plane to land.

When it did, Dessie stood up; hoping to catch a glimpse of Tasha before Tasha saw her first. Dessie watched and watched, but she didn't see anyone who even remotely resembled her friend. After the crowd thinned out a bit, both friends spotted each other at the same moment, and rushed to embrace.

"Girl look at you!" Dessie said, exploding in laughter. "Every time I see you, you have a different hairstyle! What's up with the dreads?"

"Look who's talking!" Tasha Blasted back. "What's up with the long tresses?"

"This was accidental!" Dessie said, as she lifted an end of her shoulder length hair. "I was going to have it cut for the wedding, but Mama's design for my veil requires that I have some hair to hold it up. I have to admit that it is a beautiful design, but after the first few formal photographs at the reception, I'll be taking it off."

"Did she make your dress too?"

"Now Girl you know! Ruthie was not going to be denied her honor! I picked out the design that I wanted, and Mama made it better than it actually was. I love it! Its strapless and backless."

"And she didn't have anything to say about that?"

"Now Tash, you know that it wouldn't be Ruthie if she didn't throw in her opinion!"

"But you won!" Tasha said, as she picked up her lone suitcase from the luggage conveyor.

Dessie and Tasha made small talk on the way home. Dessie wanted to reveal all the changes that had taken place in her life, but it had been so long since the two of them had been together, she decided that it was best to wait and see if they had retained the bond. "So Tash, what's going on between you and the good doctor?" Tasha sighed heavily before answering her friend.

"The good Doctor and myself are no longer together." Shocked by the revelation, Dessie implored her friend to tell her what happened.

"We moved in together, and everything was going fine until I got pregnant."

"You got what?" Dessie asked, her head spinning at hearing the news.

"Just what I said Dessie! I got pregnant! Not us; not we; I got pregnant!" Tasha started sobbing, and Dessie seeing her friend in such distress, decided that she couldn't take her home in the state she was in, and turned the car around and headed for the state park.

When Tasha's sobbing subsided a bit, she filled Dessie in on all the details that had taken place between Lance and she.

"We were living together and everything was going well. I had told him about my plans to attend medical school, and even though he wasn't crazy about it, he didn't offer any criticism towards it either. When I became pregnant, he was overjoyed at becoming a father. We made plans together, and started looking for a bigger place. After about two months, Lance came home, and as usual I had my books and papers scattered over the kitchen table. He started asking me when I was planning on stopping my studies and settle down to become a wife and mother. I was totally taken off guard by his attitude and manner of questioning me. We had a real big fight about it, and he ended up packing his things and moving out that night. After three days, I knew he wasn't coming back. Almost three months pregnant, no support from Lance, and trying to attend medical school, I had no choice but to terminate the pregnancy."

After confiding the facts to Dessie, a new onslaught of tears poured from Tasha's eyes. Dessie held onto her friend and rocked her to try and quell some of the storm inside of her. Dessie knew then that she could tell Tasha the secret that she had been keeping from everyone at home. When she told her, they both cried; for Dessie, it was out of the courage that she had to muster up to keep from killing her unborn child, and for Tasha, it was the regret of having to kill hers to spare it from a life of abandonment from a selfish father, or the unfulfilled desires of a mother who wanted both. When Tasha saw Iren's picture, his beauty overwhelmed her. She let Dessie know instantly that she was his godmother.

Leaving the park, they both somehow, felt cleansed. Tasha hadn't told her family about her pregnancy, and Dessie hadn't told her mother. The only thing that separated their stories was the fact that Dessie was determined to have her baby. Tasha knew that she would have to finish medical school now. To not do so, would have her filled with guilt for the rest of her life. She wasn't sure that she wouldn't feel that way anyhow.

Chapter Thirteen

Darryl sat inside the Shark Bar looking at a menu. He wasn't hungry, and the menu didn't tempt him to order anything. He just wanted to be done with the messy situation he was in with Troy. He hadn't planned on having to go so far to get himself clear, but he was glad that he could call on someone to help eradicate the problem.

Troy walked in as Darryl was ordering a bottle of wine dressed in all white, pants, canvas shoes, white see-thru shirt worn outside the pants. Darryl noticed that Troy's hair appeared lighter than it had earlier. *He shouldn't have on my account,* Darryl thought to himself.

"You look wonderful Troy! Have a seat." Troy wanted to sit close to Darryl so that people would think that they were a couple, but he thought better of it and sat across from him.

"Thank you for the compliment Darryl. I hoped that you would like it!" Troy smiled, showing teeth that were as white as the clothes he was wearing. A few of the other patrons stole secretive glances in their direction. Troy was like that; he always managed to turn heads wherever he happened to be. Darryl was anxious to have the evening over with and Troy permanently out of his life.

After a decent interval, Darryl whispered across to Troy to tell him what it was that he wanted from him to sever a tie that was never there, by his account, in the first place. Troy took a leisurely sip of wine; never taking his eyes off of Darryl. When he finally responded to the query, all the bitch in him seemed to spill out.

"I would love for us to get together one more time so that you will know what it is that you will be missing once our little deal is done."

"Is that all that you want..."

"Wait a minute Darryl. There's something else." Troy stood up for a split second to retrieve his wallet from his pants pocket. "I've taken the liberty of going to a car dealership of *my* choice, and selecting something that I liked. Here's the card with the salesman's name on it. He will show you just what I want." Darryl looked at the card for a moment; noticing the BMW insignia at the top of it. Darryl didn't bother looking at the location, or the name of the salesperson. He wouldn't be going there. "It's really a beauty of a car. It's a powder blue two-seat convertible. The top is navy blue. I'm going to be the envy of all my friends! I can't stop thinking about it!" gushed Troy; sounding like a schoolgirl preparing for her first real date. Darryl maintained a calm demeanor even though a slow fury was building inside of him. *When in the hell is this thing going to take place?* His mind screamed at him. He made small talk about the car to show that he was somewhat interested. Suddenly a little fury of excitement broke the calm of the moment. A beautiful woman rushed to the table where Troy and Darryl were sitting, and went straight to Darryl.

"I'm so sorry that I'm late Honey!" she said, as she bent to kiss Darryl on the lips, a little too long for Troy's comfort. "I saw these Giorgio sandals and I just had to have them for the honeymoon! Don't they look just heavenly?" the asked as she held her foot at different angles.

"Yes, they are fine," a relieved Darryl, said.

"I knew you would love them!" She said excitedly, as she bent to kiss his lips again. The woman stopped kissing Darryl for a moment and turned her attention to Troy. "Hi! Excuse me for being so rude! How do you do? My Name is Dessie," she said, "and who might you be?" she asked, as she extended her right hand to Troy who was now sitting tight-lipped through this whole production. All he could think of was that there was no way he could compete with her beauty no matter how talented his lips and tongue were. Darryl's real object of desire was right there where she stood. Troy took her hand without spirit.

"My name is Troy. I'm a friend of Darryl's."

"Oh! So you're Troy!" the woman said, "Darryl has told me so much about you!" Troy looked at Darryl in total disbelief. What could he have possibly told this woman about him and their relationship? He looked on as they shared an intimate kiss and laughter. Troy felt embarrassed by their behavior. He knew that everyone had their eyes focused on the beautiful couple sitting across from him. He didn't like the feel of this at all!

The woman reached across the table and touched Troy's hand lightly, and told him how thankful she was that he had been there for Darryl. "A lot of women would question their relationship with a guy if he were to admit something like that to their significant other's, but with Darryl and I, we have left nothing out concerning our past. Had I found out about all of this after we were married, I wouldn't have been able to keep it all together." Troy's dreams were evaporating right before his eyes. "My thing is that should he decide to go that way again, I will leave without a word." Both Darryl and the unknown woman were looking into each other eyes until their lips crushed together in a sexy, passionate kiss. When they broke apart, they saw Troy's back; shoulders slumped in defeat leaving the bar. Darryl felt a great burden lifting, as Troy seemed to get lost in the crowd. Darryl wasn't absolutely sure that it was all over; only time could tell that. But what he was feeling at that moment was something he hadn't felt in a long time.

Darryl waited a decent interval before removing an envelope from his jacket and pushing it towards the beautiful woman. She discreetly counted ten one hundred dollar bills, and smilingly told him that it was a shame to let the evening go to waste after he had paid such a high price for it. She massaged his thick penis under the table. "I can feel why fag boy wanted to hold onto to you!" Darryl laughed as he lifted his glass in one hand to his lips, while removing her hand from his dick with the other. He thanked her for her services as he got up to leave the bar. Alone.

Chapter Fourteen

After the rehearsal, which went off without a hitch, a small motorcade wound it's way to Ruthie's. A few missionaries from the church had been there from late in the afternoon to the present.

Ruthie showed them a rehearsal dinner the likes of which they had never seen before. Not only was there food inside, but there was food outside as well. Ruthie had ordered a whole pig butchered. Most of it had been slow grilled earlier. The aroma of the sauce could be smelled up and down the block. Ruthie wanted the wedding party and immediate guest to have a memorable meal. She sure didn't think the meal that was to be served after the wedding would have anyone remembering anything at all about it: Baked chicken, wild rice, with asparagus tips and green salad. *If that was the way New York people ate, then a real meal like hers would kill them!* Ruthie thought to herself.

Darryl's first introduction to his perspective mother-in-law was thirty minutes after he had been in her home. Every time Dessie tried to get the two together, Ruthie was needed somewhere else. Dessie became busy and Darryl felt abandoned. When she went looking for him, he was nowhere to be found. Just as Dessie was about to go outside to look for him, Ruthie exited her bedroom with Darryl right behind her as she dabbed her eyes with her handkerchief. Dessie instantly thought that something was wrong. Darryl started smiling immediately;

letting Dessie know that there was nothing to fear. "What's the matter Mama?" Dessie asked.

"It's nothing Baby. Darryl just asked my permission to take your hand in marriage, and it reminded me of the time your daddy asked my daddy for my hand," Ruthie said as she wiped fresh tears from her eyes. "You have a good man Dessie, and I already know that he's gonna be a good son-in-law. Dessie hugged her mother thinking that life had been forgiving and rewarding.

DC

Tasha and Dessie retreated to her bedroom for the rest of the evening as Ruthie put some finishing touches on Tasha's dress. Darryl and the others had gone back to the hotel to get some rest; that Dessie knew wasn't going to happen because the mood of the group was far too festive to seriously consider getting some rest. Dessie made Darryl promise that he would stay at the hotel and not go out on the town should his groomsmen choose to do so.

Once inside Dessie's old bedroom, Tasha's sadness quickly came out. "I wish that I had did what you did Dessie. I wish that I had kept my baby even if I had to go it alone.

"Our circumstances were very different Tasha. You didn't have the support that I had. Women have such a hard way to go when we feel that our options are limited."

"You hit the nail right on the head!" Tasha responded. "There have never been that many outlets for women in trouble. If I had chosen to have my baby, I might have condemned us to a life of poverty. I know that I would have had to put my plans on a back burner; hoping to someday be able to pick them back up. I just didn't have the support that you had Dessie. Had it been there, maybe the outcome of my situation would have been different."

"Tash, do you remember the night of the debutante ball?" Dessie asked.

"Yeah. What about it?"

"Remember what the guest speaker said about her situation? She said that after all she had gone through, that she never once wished that she was someone else, or that her circumstances were different. Tasha nodded her head up and down. Her best friend had just uttered the words that she needed to hear. She could go on with her life now, and stop wallowing in self-pity. Charlene's problems came rushing in at that very moment when she decided to let hers go.

"Charlene is pregnant again!" Tasha blurted out. Dessie stopped packing her suitcase as she digested the news.

"So that's why we haven't seen Charlene! I've been so busy with the wedding that I've clean forgotten about my sister-in-law. Clanford and she must be very happy with their growing family!"

"Clanford doesn't know anything about it, and Charlene isn't happy at all. In fact, she's damn near suicidal!" Dessie looked at Tasha in total disbelief.

"I believe that Charlene is suffering from depression, and she's been like this since the last baby was born. Next week, we are taking her to see a new doctor. I don't think that she'll be at the wedding."

"I saw Clanford and I didn't even think to ask him about Charlene." Dessie lamented.

"Clanford is hardly ever at home now. Charlene says that he is always away on church business, and that some of the members of the congregation are always calling him at all hours of the night, needing help with children or husbands. Charlene said that most of the calls come from single women, and when she brought the matter up, he told her to stop assuming that something other than counseling and prayer was going on. Now when the phone rings in the middle of the night, Clanford makes sure that he is the one that answers it." Dessie couldn't utter a word after hearing what Tasha had to say. She thought about the things she had done with Ray, and her heart started to break for Charlene.

"I hope that what you are insinuating is not happening Tasha. We don't need to have any more situations like that happening in this family," Dessie said.

"Dessie please don't mention anything about it. Charlene is too fragile to stand up against the gossip. My mother has been staying with her as much as possible since she's been in this latest decline. Mama said that the other day when she got there, Charlene was just sitting on the side of the bed while the baby screamed to be fed, and the phone ringing; she just sat there looking straight ahead. We have got to get her some help!"

Dessie knew right at that moment that she was no longer going to work towards a law degree. She felt that she was being called to action on the behalf of women that were often caught just like Tasha and Charlene was; the way that she had been. Women needed powerful, as well as positive solutions to a barrage of complicated problems that hindered their economic and mental growth. Dessie decided to look into pursuing a course of study that would better equip her to be of service and resource to those who needed it the most. Her decision made her feel vital and important.

As Dessie drifted off into a tired sleep, she could hear the sound of thunder in the distance. She thought that she mouthed the phrase *'Happy is the bride that it rains on her wedding day.'* If she didn't say them; at least she thought that she had.

&#x0001;C

Early morning showers followed the late night rain that bought out the best nature had to offer in lush greenery, beautiful wildflowers, and carefully tended gardens of all types. A lovelier day could not have been wished for.

Ruthie had Dessie and Tasha up by seven thirty, a half hour later than she had intended, but she knew that they had talked late into the night and needed the rest.

Ruthie fixed them a very light breakfast of fruit, toast and tea. She knew that they were going to be too excited to really eat anything. Plus, she knew that neither wanted that full, sluggish feeling.

Promptly at ten, a silver limousine arrived to take them to the church. Ruthie and Tasha were already dressed, and Dessie had her hair and make up finished, but she wouldn't get dressed until she arrived at the church.

The photographer had been at the house to take some photographs of them preparing to leave for the church. The one that Dessie thought she would love the best was the one that he took of Ruthie and she at the vanity in Ruthie's bedroom with Ruthie fixing Dessie's hair, and making sure that it worked with her veil. It was a photograph that said this is the way things should be. Mother helping daughter prepare for her biggest day ever. It couldn't be more personal than it was right now. The photographer left them to rush off to the hotel to catch the guys in their final stages of preparations.

Dessie and all of her bridesmaids, along with her mother, helped her get dressed in the spacious dressing room of the church. Every one of them were speechless as she stood in front of the full-length mirror to check her appearance. She looked like a different person in her splendor. All eyes were moist with tears at the resplendent sight of the beautiful bride.

Shortly afterwards, Brent knocked on the door telling Ruthie that it was time for her to take her place. She hugged Dessie and rushed out of the dressing room. Clanford was standing in the vestibule waiting with the groomsmen. Soon, it was time for Dessie to take her place. A white runner extended from the entrance of the sanctuary to the alter. The sight was breathtaking. The church was filled with flowers; all tied with bunches of pink satin ribbons. Darlene certainly kept her word on how beautiful she and her staff could make this whole production.

Trumpets sounded announcing the beginning of the ceremony, and everyone stood in honor of the bride. Clanford looked like an elegant movie star in his dress whites with black tails. Dessie could understand why so many women found him irresistible-even if he was forbidden fruit! He was the perfect stand-in for their father.

When Dessie saw Darryl standing at the alter, her heart leaped with the love that was in her for him. When Clanford delivered her to him, he bowed deeply just as they had rehearsed. She felt like a queen as Darryl pulled her close, clasping her dainty hands in his comforting, strong masculine ones. As the service moved on, just before they were to take their vows, the minister stopped speaking and sort of smiled at the couple. There was a little flurry of activity, and suddenly the church was filled with the sound of stringed instruments. Someone moved into position in front of a standing microphone and started to sing. Dessie remembered the song and the distinct voice. She looked at the singer and could not contain a gasp as she squeezed Darryl's hand. "That's...

"Yes Honey, it is him." Darryl whispered. Those that were sitting in the rear, stood to get a better view of the singer.

"He use to sing with that group...

"Yes he did." Darryl whispered.

"But how could you manage...

"My dad did some legal work for him some years ago and we've stayed in touch." Darryl whispered to her as they were swept away by the magic of *'For The Lover In You.'* Dessie looked over at her friends, and was not surprised to see Sharon fanning a swooning Debra. She looked up into Darryl's eyes, and eschewing tradition, she kissed her first love a little too long, prompting Clanford to remind the couple that they still had to take their vows.

DC

One of the most memorable moments at the reception was when Brent sang *'With You I'm Born Again.'* Dessie told him again that he should pursue a singing career. He didn't realize just how great his voice was.

Dessie and Darryl took a short plane ride to Orlando. Darryl had wanted to honeymoon out of the country, but with the international strife going on, staying close to home was the best choice.

Once they arrived at the airport, Dessie wanted to call Etta and see how everything was going with Iren, but Darryl persuaded her to wait so that they wouldn't miss their flight. Dessie was a little bit upset about not being able to speak to Iren and Etta, but Darryl promised that the moment that they arrived at the hotel, she could call and talk to Iren and Etta as long as she liked.

They picked up the car at the rental counter in the airport and headed for the Hyatt Regency on International Drive where they were to spend a week. Darryl went to park the car while Dessie followed their luggage into the hotel lobby to check in and get the keys to their suite. She was standing at the counter when she heard a tiny voice call out 'Mommy.' Dessie thought that she had heard her baby's voice, but she passed it off as her mind playing tricks on her. She had wanted to talk to him so badly earlier till she was now thinking that he was calling out to her. She heard the tiny voice call out 'Mommy' again. This time sounding as if he was about to cry. Dessie turned to see where the little voice was coming from, and almost screamed out at the sight of Etta holding the tiny hand of her beautiful son. She rushed over grabbing both of them as best she could. She couldn't contain the tears of happiness that coursed down her cheeks, begging Etta to tell her how and why they were there.

"Your new husband flew us down here yesterday. He wanted to surprise you." At that moment, Darryl entered the lobby and walked directly to his family, embracing them at once.

"Honey you are amazing!" Dessie said through tears, "How did you know that I wanted to see my son so badly?"

"I knew that you wanted to see *our* son, so I arranged for Etta and Iren to be here when we checked in. I want us to have a real family vacation."

"Thank you so much Honey," Dessie, said softly in Darryl's ear, "I'm so proud to be your wife."

"And I want you to be mine forever!" Darryl said as they got on the elevator to go up to their rooms.

Three Years Later

I see the head Honey! I can see it! It's almost over now Sweetheart!" Darryl said to an extremely tired Dessie.

"Honey, you already know that 'it' is a girl. Why don't you say 'she' or call her by her name?"

"I'm sorry Honey. Deirdre is almost here. One more push and you can relax. It'll be all over." Dessie was so tired; all she wanted to do was go to sleep and be away from the pain of birthing. Comparing the two labors she'd endured, this one was a piece cake compared to that of Iren's, but she still hurt and wanted it over. Another contraction hit and Dessie bore down, squeezing Darryl's hand so hard that his fingertips were white due to the decrease of blood flow. A scream caught in Dessie's throat and Deirdre came into the world at three twenty five a.m. She was quickly wiped down and placed in Dessie's arms.

"She is so Beautiful Honey!" Darryl exclaimed. Dessie tenderly stroked her baby's head.

"Look at our poor little daughter Darryl! She doesn't have any hair!" was all Dessie would say as she smiled down on the small miracle angelically looking back at her.

"She is perfect for us," Darryl said, gently kissing his tired wife as their daughter held onto his finger.

Six Months Later...

"Dessie you need to come home now." Darryl said into the receiver.

"Honey I can't! I have a sixteen-year-old client coming in, and she will only talk to me. I tried to get her to talk to another counselor, but she said that they couldn't possibly understand what's going on in her head if they don't live where she lives. No amount of reassurance can get her to change her mind."

Ever since her marriage, Dessie has worked to empower women on basic issues in their lives. In two years, she earned an advanced degree in women studies, and continues to attend seminars and workshops pertaining to the development and advancement of all women.

When she began to equip herself to deal with issues concerning women, her focus was primarily on minority women, but as she soon learned, women all over the world were being adversely affected by decisions of not only their husbands and boyfriends, but governments as well. A sixteen-year-old motherless child, living with her twenty two year old boyfriend, pressuring her to quit school and seek employment to make life easier for them was just one of the issues that Dessie had been dealing with over the past two weeks, but probably, the most minor. Darryl waited until Dessie had stopped talking. He knew that trying to get her to listen to him when she was so involved was useless. His silence let her know that what he had to say was serious.

"What is it Darryl? Are the children okay?" Dessie asked, almost in a panic.

"The children are fine, but I need for you to come home now Dessie." The sober way that he was speaking let Dessie know that an issue was brewing that needed her attention.

"I'll cancel my appointments, and you can send the sitter home."

"She's already gone. I paid her for the rest of the week also." Dessie didn't find that unusual. Both of them would often pay their babysitter in advance, but would let the other know that they had done so, so that they didn't issue duplicate checks for the same week.

DC

When Dessie arrived home, Iren ran to hug her before she could her coat off. "What are you doing home so early today young man?" Dessie asked her son in a authoritative voice; which caused Iren to giggle musically.

"Daddy said that I'm special and I get to leave school early today." Iren explained, as Dessie stroked his full head of beautiful black curls.

"And where is Daddy?"

"He's fixing my lunch in the kitchen."

"What happened to the lunch that I fixed this morning?"

"I ate it, but I was still hungry and Daddy said he would make me another sandwich." Dessie didn't have to ask him what kind of sandwich Darryl was making because from the time he was three years old; he hadn't eaten anything for lunch except peanut butter and jelly with three cookies for dessert. At first she was alarmed that he might not be getting all the nutrients that he needed, but his pediatrician assured her that all was fine and his development was above average.

"Hi Honey," Darryl said, appearing in the living room drying his hands on a paper towel. "Iren your sandwich is on the table," Darryl said, looking seriously at Dessie. As Iren ran to eat his sandwich, Darryl turned his attention to his wife. "Dessie, Honey, your brother called this morning. Your mother went into the hospital last night." Hearing those words, Dessie seemed to fall back on the sofa; too weak to continue to stand. Darryl sat next to her holding her hand as he continued. "Clanford said that the doctor thinks that she had a heart attack. She's really in bad shape right now. You have to get there right away." Dessie jumped up, pressing her fingers against her temples.

"I have a thousand things to do," She said more to herself than to Darryl, "I have to call an airline to arrange for a flight out as soon as possible, I have to get the children packed. Honey can you see if you can get seating on a plane for the kids and myself?" Dessie asked, wondering where and what should she start packing.

"It's already taken care of Dessie. I've arranged for us to leave New York at seven this evening."

"Us?" Dessie asked in a bewildered tone.

"You didn't think that I was going to let you go by yourself did you?"

"But whose going to handle your affairs Darryl while we are gone?"

"Don't worry about that Honey. The few criminal cases that I have, I've already gotten continuances on, and anything else, my partners and secretary are well equipped to deal with whatever comes up." Dessie laid her head on his chest and cried; thanking him for being the person that he was.

𝒟𝒞

It's funny how hope means so much to you when you've been told that there is nothing else. These were Dessie's thoughts as she moved towards her mother's hospital room. She will never forget the way that the young female doctor used her hands to show her how a heart was supposed to beat, and with the same hands, showed her how her mother's was barely functioning. Dessie wanted to grab the doctor's hands and spring life back into the description of her mother's heart. She suddenly felt angry with the doctor, and quickly realized that she had already begun the grieving process. *First the anger.* As the doctor continued to elaborate on Ruthie's deteriorating condition, she lifted a sleeping Deirdre out of Darryl's arms, and took Iren by the hand and silently walked the few steps that it took to get to her mother's bedside.

Stunned at first by all the monitors and intravenous lines, Dessie couldn't move towards the bed, and as if he had been summoned, Darryl appeared at her side; gently taking Deirdre from her increasingly tiring arms. Still holding onto Iren's trembling hand, she moved over to Ruthie's bedside. Looking down on her mother, all Dessie could think was that her mother was not that old. She was old in ways, but not in days. Dessie took hold of Ruthie's hand and found that it was cool to the touch. She made a mental note to tell the nurse at the desk to bring in another blanket. As she held her mama's hand, Ruthie opened her eyes.

"What you doing here Baby?"

"They told us you were sick Mama, and we came right away."

"Aw shoot! I'm just a little tired. That's all. Wasn't no need for you to come all this way just for that," she said weakly. "Who is that pretty little thing that you got there?" With tears streaming down her cheeks, Dessie brought Iren as close to the bed as she could.

"He's mine Mama. When I left here after Junie Boy was killed, I was pregnant."

"Why didn't you tell me Child?" Ruthie weakly asked.

"I was scared Mama. So much shame had already come to this family, I couldn't bear to bring anymore hurt on you."

"Child, you wouldn't have brought no such thing! A child is a blessing from God. And another thing, love covers a multitude of sin." Ruthie reached out to stroke Iren's thick black curls. "Lord you sure is pretty! Gram got her a pretty grandbaby! I can't wait until I get out of here cause Grandma is going to make you something pretty. Something pretty for my pretty grandbaby." Ruthie took Dessie's hand and thanked her for coming. "I always had a feeling that something was missing, and I couldn't quite figure out what it was, but now I know, and that old feeling is gone. Dessie Lee, I'm getting so tired now, ya'll go on to the house and get some rest. Ya'll come and see me tomorrow when I ain't so tired." Ruthie closed her eyes and her hand felled heavily from Dessie's. The heart monitor above the bed went from bumps and ridges, to a solid white, flat line. It took Dessie a couple of seconds to realize what had just happened. When she did, her screams brought hospital personnel from every direction.

Before leaving the hospital, Darryl demanded that Dessie be given a sedative. Without it, he wasn't sure that her mind could handle the loss.

𝒟𝒞

Debutantes from the last twenty years to the present, were in attendance to pay homage to a fallen queen. They came from all parts of the world; doctors, lawyers, teachers, judges-every profession under the sun was represented. Husbands were in tow with children, but as if told beforehand, stayed pretty much in the background. Woman after woman came to the podium to bestow upon Ruthie all the virtues of becoming a debutante. Dr. LaTasha Wright gave the eulogy. She spoke on how important it was that as a child, you had to be careful about what you did because every mother and father were equal to your own and carried the same power as such. Quite a few women chuckled when Tasha described what happened when you rang Ruthie's doorbell a little too long.

Brent saluted his aunt with one of her favorite songs, *'When My Work Is All Done.'* All in attendance felt the tears that fell from his eyes. As he moved from the alter to the center aisle, he continued to sing the mournful lyrics, exiting the church, where his voice unaccompanied by musical instruments, sounded like an angel singing to the glory that he had witnessed.

Ruthie was laid to rest on a hill in the cemetery on the right of Desmond. It was where she had wanted to be. She had long understood the power of forgiveness. Dessie was comforted knowing that her mother was now, safely home.

195

Ten Years Later

"Iren! For the last time, you better get your narrow behind out of that bed!" Dessie yelled from the foot of the stairs before going back into the kitchen. A few minutes later, Dessie could hear his heavy footsteps on the carpeted stairs.

"What do you want Ma?" an annoyed Iren asked Dessie's back. Dessie turned around to face her handsome, tall son.

"I want you to..." Dessie stopped speaking in mid sentence when she saw how her son was dressed, or *undressed*. "Iren, how many times do I have to tell you about walking around here in nothing but your underwear? You are way too big for that now."

"Ma, I have on my boxers! They are just like shorts."

"And they can't hide nothing! What if one of your aunties were over and saw you looking like that? What do you think they'll say?"

"Thank you Lord! My prayers have been answered?"

"Don't play with me Boy!" Dessie instructed, throwing a wet sponge at her first born who was laughing his head off. "I want you to get dressed and take Deirdre over to the park so that she can ride her bike."

"Aw Ma! Why do I have to take her? I wanted to sleep late today!"

"If you would stay off that phone all hours of the night..." Dessie stopped talking and closed her eyes. In a moment, her cheeks were moist. Iren looked at her and put his arms around her.

"What's the matter Ma? You know that I'll take her to the park."

"That's not it Baby. I just remembered something from a long time ago." Iren looked at her for a long moment before speaking.

"I don't think I'm ever going to understand you women." He went and got dressed to take Deirdre to the park. Before he left the house, he slipped a small notepad and pen in the back pocket of a snug pair of jeans.

SHOUT-OUTS
Thank You

Terrell Bush for keeping me fed!
Solomon Cicero for the technology and friendship.
Vernell Cohen for the class, style and sexiness!
Robin Allen for keeping me busy!
Doris Price for keeping it real, up front, and in your "Face"!
Marcia Brookins for the compassion.
Sheila Francis for keeping me humble and patient!
Carolyn Lee for keeping me in the library and kitchen!
Lorraine Wonza for keeping me going, and sane!
Kathleen Register for keeping the knowledge.
Patricia Washington for keeping me determined.
Lou Oliver for keeping me aware.
Loytoya Williams for reminding me of home.
Nicolas Jones Jr. for keeping me a leader.
George Cruz for keeping me searching.
Monique James for the "facetyness"!
Tascha Fitzpatrick for keeping the artist in me.
Lenore Jackson for keeping me focused.
Larry Manning Jr. For keeping me company.
Tarshea Jordan for keeping me safe.
Annie McGhee, Sheila Marchand, Leverne Pennycooke for keeping the child in me.
Cheryl Young for keeping the discipline.
Jeremy Osterling for keeping the music in me.
Harrison George for keeping a second chance.
Sylvia Fagan for listening.
Louis Navarro for always helping.

COMING SOON!!

An inheritance placed into the hands of those without
Knowledge or work ethics is pure disaster.

ONE

"You gonna let me or what?"

"Or what?"

"Yeah. Or *what?* Either we do it or we don't."

"But you know that I'm a virgin Iren. I'm not ready to be just another conquest for you. Everybody knows your reputation.

"Everybody *thinks* that they know it, but I'm the only one that truly knows me." Iren said, nuzzling the ear of the girl he had asked out at lunch. She was being tough. He usually had the drawers off by now. *I must be slipping*, he thought to himself. He covered her mouth with his own, catching her off

guard. She laid her head back on the headrest. His kisses had her on the verge of fainting, or so she thought. "Your kisses are making me dizzy Iren," she said.

"It's not my kisses that'll have your head spinning!" when he spoke those words, she started pulling at his shirt; trying to draw him closer to her. He knew that he had made it to where he wanted to be. There would be no stopping her now. His work was done. He could lay back and enjoy the ride. He never had to work too hard to get 'some.' Girls and women threw themselves at him all the time. Sometimes he took it, sometimes he didn't. his looks were able to take him places money never would. At seventeen, he already had had more women than most men twice his age. They had taught him the things that he needed to know. He knew how to take a woman to the brink of pure ecstasy, and hold back long enough to have her whimpering with unsatisfied desire.

She was now out of the passenger seat straddling his thighs; as she unbuttoned his shirt. He may have been only seventeen, but he had the body of a man. A very beautiful man. She ran her fingers over his virile chest; fascinated by the wisps of hair on it as she kissed his exciting lips. He had her bra off of her a full five minutes before she even realized it. His expert tongue had her naked breast doing a dance of their own. She could feel him, and she knew that what all the other girls had talked about was true. By him picking her, he had to feel something for her. Right? Since she'd entered high school, and seen Iren pinning a girl to her locker and kissing her as if they were the only ones in the hall. She never thought that there was a chance that she would get with him, but here she was, in his car, half undressed; her pleated uniform skirt bunched around her waist. "Take your panties off," Iren said between nibbles at her lips. She maneuvered herself back into the passenger seat; sliding her panties to the floor as Iren undid his pants and stroked himself. She looked at what he held in his hand and almost changed her mind. He saw the look of astonishment on her face and told her not to worry about it, and that he always kept some lubricant to help ease the insertion. He handed her a latex condom and told her to put it on him.

Using both hands, she managed to get him somewhat covered, and herself hotter than she had ever known possible. She was scared, but she wanted to please him in every way that she could. He told her to get on top of him again and positioned the head of his swollen penis at her opening. Heat emanating from him seemed to gather in one spot and she was going to devour the whole thing at once. She bore down hard and was back off of him in half a second. "You can't do it like that yet," Iren cautioned her. "You have to work your way down." He took the very large head and slowly rubbed her tight vagina with it until he could feel her loosening up and getting wetter. "Now you should be able to take a little in," Iren huskily said, anticipating her tightness. Fearfully, she brought her opening into contact with his rigid member. She did as he had instructed her, and it was easier. Along with the lubrication and her own juices, she succeeded in getting just past the head. He cautioned her not to think that that was it. He hadn't moved one inch since she started her descent. He let her control everything. He knew that when he did start thrusting, it would be almost more than she could stand. His main concern was not bursting the condom. He was already at risk. The damn things only fit halfway down his shaft because he was so wide. The few times that he had had unprotected sex, were fantastic, but each time had been with much older women who were on the pill or used some other contraceptive method where all he had to worry about was tiring his partner out before the fun really began.

When he wanted some quick relief, he would always call on the experienced ones. When he wanted to have fun, just for the hell of it, he found him one that was not too hard to look at, but lacking self confidence. He could have his way those, and they would never know the difference. Just like this one, trying to take as much of him as she could. *Just wait until I go to work. She'll either follow me around like a puppy, or run the other way when she sees me coming.* Iren thought.

Iren used his tongue on her nipples expertly. When it was time, he grabbed her hips and brought them down hard onto his lap. A scream started then stopped as if it was caught in her throat. Her mouth remained open as he tore into her. She felt like she was ripped apart. Nothing would be able to put her back together again. She tried to struggle off him, but the more she moved, the more excited he became and held her firmly in place. Soon, she too was caught up in the pleasure he was bringing. This was beyond anything that she had ever thought about. With an orgasm quickly approaching, she pulled on his hair as if she was about to drown and only his hair could save her. When it hit, screams came from so deep inside of her, she didn't know that it was she who made the sounds. He had held off his own orgasm to make sure that she felt the full impact of all that he had done to her. He made sure that she would always remember him-even if he forgot her.

When he was about to reach his peak, he whispered in her ear that he was about to come, and his hot breath on her ear seemed to bring on another knee-weakening orgasm. Not as shattering as the first, but still powerful enough to cause her to cry. Staying inside of her for a few minutes longer, when he started pulling himself out of her, she came again; begging him to stop before he killed her. "I've never heard of two healthy people dying from having an orgasm before!" he said.

"I'm sure that it could happen. I've never felt anything like that in my entire life."

"That's cause you've never been with me before. I aim to please," Iren said, as he zipped up his pants. He reached into the glove compartment and retrieved several moist towel packets; giving her several.

"I love you Iren, and I want to be yours."

"Why?" he asked.

"No one else has made me feel the way you have."

"Could that be because you haven't been with anybody else?"

"I'm not talking about *that* Iren! I've gone out with other guys. None of them made me feel the way you did. The first time I saw you, I dreamed of being your girlfriend. I didn't think you would ever notice me. I went to all your home games hoping that you would notice me. It seemed like every girl there was trying to do the same thing: to get you to look at them!"

"You can't make me believe that every girl that comes to the games come to see me."

"Most of them did," she said, trying to comb her back into the style that she had it in before their tryst. "But I'm the one that you got with. They are going to so jealous when I tell them that you and I are going together." Iren stopped wiping his hands and looked at the girl sitting next to him.

"What are you talking about Terry?" he questioned.

"Terry? Who are you talking to Iren?" Taken off guard, Iren didn't make an attempt to correct his mistake. He didn't know what her name was.

"Since you don't know it, or can't remember it, the name is 'Tracey!' I can't believe that we just

made love and you can't even remember my name," she said, with slight indignation.

"Hey, I'll take that. That's on me, but what is this stuff about us 'making love?' The one thing

that I do remember is that we fucked! Plain and simple. That's all we did!"

"I thought you said we were going to be together."

"I *said* you could always get with me if you wanted to. Man, I can't be responsible for what you heard!"

"You can take me home now Iren!" Tracey said through tears, without looking at the boy who had just deflowered her.

Iren drove her to her building with the stereo in the car blasting; eliminating the need for conversation. When she exited the car, she gave him a hard, disenchanted look.

"I'll hit you up later," he said, uncomfortably, and pulled away from the curb leaving her standing.